The Great Return

The Great Return

Emigrants, come home!

Paul Weatherdon

Copyright © 2024 the Author

All rights reserved

ISBN: 9798335553605

The author is contactable on X

@PaulWeatherdon

Dedication

For my son

Dedicated to the hope that the principle of
jus sanguinis - the law of bloodline - will be embraced in the UK, enabling the return of her people from across the globe to their rightful home

Prologue

Be careful what you wish for.

It began as a whisper, a murmur of change that rippled through the corridors of power and across the vast landscapes of a world on the brink. By 2027, the concept of globalisation—once hailed as the great equaliser—had begun to crumble under the weight of its own contradictions. The promises of interconnected prosperity had given way to a reality marked by deepening inequality, cultural dislocation, and the erosion of national identities. The backlash was inevitable.

Outside of Europe and the USA, vast powers had aligned. The Global Mega Union (GMU), an alliance of the world's most populous non-'Western' nations, had emerged from the economic might of the new global order. Comprising countries that had long been considered the future engines of growth, the GMU represented 70% of the world's population, a formidable bloc united by a shared vision of a different kind of globalisation—one that placed the interests of the majority above the elites of the West.

The GMU's leaders, driven by a growing sense of injustice and a desire to reshape the world according to their values, declared that the time had come to right the wrongs of history. They argued that globalisation had failed, that it had stripped nations of their sovereignty, eroded the fabric of societies, and left billions in the grip of poverty and despair. And so, they proposed a radical solution: to reverse the tide of history and restore the world to its natural order.

The announcement sent shockwaves across the globe. The GMU called for the dismantling of the structures of globalisation and the repatriation of all people to their countries of ancestral origin—a return to the lands of their DNA. The message was clear: the age of mass migration was over, and the time had come for humanity to return home.

For the United States, it meant a future where the only people left were the indigenous tribes who had once roamed the land before the arrival of European settlers. Australia would be a land of the Aboriginal peoples, South Africa would see the departure of its white minority, and Europe, particularly the United Kingdom, would face the unprecedented challenge of welcoming back hundreds of millions of people with British DNA from across the world.

The United Kingdom, the epicentre of this seismic shift, was uniquely unprepared for the upheaval that followed. A nation that had once colonised much of the world was now faced with the task of accommodating those who had spread across the globe in search of new lives. The Global Repatriation Act, passed in the wake of the GMU's declaration, mandated the return of all those with majority British DNA. It was a logistical and social challenge of unimaginable proportions, and it threatened to tear the very fabric of the nation apart.

In cities and towns across the UK, the effects of The Great Return were felt immediately. London, once a beacon of multiculturalism, became a melting pot of cultural and historical identities, as millions of people returned to the land of their ancestors. The streets were filled with voices speaking in accents from every corner of the globe, as people who had never set foot in England struggled to find their place in a country that was both foreign and familiar.

But The Great Return was more than just a demographic shift—it was a reckoning with history. The returnees brought with them the legacies of colonialism, migration, and displacement, and their presence forced the country to confront the unresolved issues of its past. The questions of what it meant to be English, of who belonged and who did not, were thrust into the forefront of the national conversation.

As the country grappled with these questions, another force was quietly gaining power. The Consortium, a shadowy network of corporate and political interests, saw in The Great Return an opportunity to exploit the chaos for their own gain. They fanned the flames of division, using nationalist rhetoric to manipulate public opinion and tighten their grip on power. The returnees, many of whom had come to England with dreams of a better life, quickly found themselves scapegoated, caught in the crossfire of a battle for the nation's soul.

It was in this climate of fear and uncertainty that the story of The Great Return unfolded. It is a story of resilience and hope, of ordinary people rising to the challenge of extraordinary times. It is a story of justice and reconciliation, of a country confronting the darkest chapters of its history and striving to build a better future.

As the echoes of tomorrow began to reverberate through the world of 2027, no one could have predicted the profound impact The Great Return would have on the course of history. But as the events of that year would soon prove, the future is shaped by the choices we make in the face of the unknown.

And in the United Kingdom, the choices made in the coming days, weeks, and months would determine not only the fate of a nation but the very future of what it meant to be human in a world that was rapidly changing beyond recognition.

Contents

The Return Begins	15
Tensions Rising	25
The Underbelly	45
The Shifting Sands	55
The Gathering Storm	63
Shadows in the Streets	71
Fractures in the Foundation	79
Lines Drawn in the Sand	87
The Turning Point	95
Resilience in the Shadows	103
The Final Push	111
Aftermath	119
Rebuilding Trust	127
New Beginnings	135
The Gathering Strength	143
The Road Ahead	151
The Reckoning	157
Epilogue: The Legacy of The Great Return	165

1

THE RETURN BEGINS

The announcement came on an ordinary day, with the mundane rhythm of life carrying on as it had always done. But the words that crackled through the airwaves and lit up screens across the globe were anything but ordinary. The Global Mega Union (GMU) had made its decision, and there would be no turning back.

In England, the response was immediate and visceral. For decades, the country had wrestled with questions of identity, immigration, and belonging. Now, those questions were thrust into the forefront of national consciousness in a way that no one could ignore. The government, caught off guard by the GMU's decree, scrambled to formulate a response, but the truth was that no one was prepared for what was coming.

In the heart of London, Sarah James watched the news unfold from the comfort of her flat, her mind reeling with the implications. She had always considered herself English, despite the traces of her ancestors' journeys that wound through her DNA. Born and raised in London, Sarah was a product of the city's diverse tapestry—a blend of cultures, histories, and identities that had shaped her into who she was.

But now, as she listened to the pundits and politicians debate the logistics of The Great Return, Sarah felt a growing sense of unease. What did it mean to be English in this new world? Could a nation built on centuries of migration and empire truly absorb the return of so many? And where did she fit into all of this?

The government's initial response was to focus on logistics—housing, employment, social services. But beneath the surface, deeper questions were beginning to bubble up. What would happen to the fragile balance of English society when millions of returnees arrived, each with their own expectations, their own needs, and their own interpretations of what it meant to be English?

The streets of London, always teeming with life, began to feel more crowded, more tense. Conversations that had once been polite or avoided altogether now spilled into the open, fuelled by fear, anger, and uncertainty. For some, The Great Return was seen as a chance to reclaim a lost sense of identity, a return to a purer, more authentic England. For others, it was a nightmare—a forced collision of worlds that could only end in chaos.

As the days passed, the first waves of returnees began to

arrive. Airports were filled with people clutching documents, their faces a mix of hope and trepidation. Some were returning to family homes, places their ancestors had left generations before. Others had no ties to the land at all, their connection to England little more than a name on a document or a distant memory passed down through stories.

Sarah watched these arrivals with a sense of growing dread. The city she loved was changing, and she wasn't sure if it was for the better. But there was no time for hesitation. As a journalist, Sarah knew that she had a role to play in documenting this moment in history, in capturing the stories of those who were being swept up in this unprecedented movement of people.

She began to immerse herself in the unfolding drama, interviewing returnees, local residents, and officials who were struggling to keep up with the demands of the new reality. What she found was a city—and a country—on the brink. The returnees were not just bringing their belongings; they were bringing their cultures, their histories, and their expectations of what life in England should be.

For some, the return was a dream fulfilled—a chance to reconnect with their roots and build a new life in a land they had always considered home, even if they had never set foot on its soil. For others, it was a bewildering ordeal, a journey into the unknown where the promise of a better life was overshadowed by the challenges of integration and acceptance.

In one of her first interviews, Sarah spoke with Jenny Howard, a returnee who had come from Sydney, a city now left desolate, with only people of Aboriginal DNA allowed to move in. Jenny's story was one of contrasts. Born and raised in Australia, she had always known about her English ancestry, but it had been little more than a curiosity, a distant connection to a land she had never seen. The announcement of The Great Return had changed everything. Jenny was among the first to be remigrated (a new word explaining this affects emigrants, not merely expatriates who would normally at the end of their expatriate term, repatriate). Remigration was ordered by the GMU based on the DNA tests of every living person, the logistics were handled by the country the returnee was being remigrated to. The beach cottage she owned in Bali had been taken away from her, but she was awarded a market price, of 3.5 Billion Indonesian Rupiahs. In an effort to equalise currencies, the GMU introduced 'ecoins' which they decreed would be equal, one to one of all local currencies. This meant that Jenny was suddenly a Billionaire in the UK, just as countries with low currency value, suddenly had large parts of their populations becoming millionaires, in ecoins. Everyone except people in strong currency countries, were delighted!

"It's strange," Jenny said during their interview, her voice filled with a mix of wonder and apprehension. "I've always felt a connection to England, but it was more like a dream than anything real. And now, here I am, back in the land of my ancestors, trying to figure out how I fit into this place. The money helps, of course, but it also makes things more complicated. People look at me differently, and I'm not sure if it's because of my background or because of the wealth that came with it."

Sarah listened, sensing the layers of complexity in Jenny's experience. Here was a woman who, despite her newfound wealth, was navigating the same uncertainties as thousands of other returnees. The money might have eased some practical concerns, but it hadn't answered the deeper questions of identity and belonging.

As Sarah continued her work, she encountered stories that were both heartwarming and heartbreaking. There was George Hayes, an elderly man in Manchester whose family had lived in England for generations. The return of so many people with English DNA was, to him, a mixed blessing. He welcomed the idea of reconnecting with distant relatives and seeing the country filled with those who shared his heritage. But he also worried about the strain it would place on an already fragile society.

"My father used to tell me stories about our family's roots in England," George said, his voice tinged with nostalgia. "But those roots have been stretched across the world. Now they're coming back, and I'm not sure what that means for us. I want to believe it's a good thing, but I can't shake the feeling that we're on the edge of something we don't fully understand."

In Birmingham, Sarah met with a group of young returnees who were struggling to find their place in schools that were suddenly overcrowded and under-resourced. Among them was Emma White, a bright and ambitious teenager who had spent her early years in India. Despite her English ancestry, Emma found herself feeling like an outsider in a country that was supposed to be her home.

"The kids here—they look like me, but they don't see me as one of them," Emma confessed, her eyes downcast. "They call me a foreigner, even though I'm as English as they are. It's hard, trying to fit in when you feel like you're constantly being judged. I just want to belong, but I don't know how."

These stories painted a picture of a nation in flux, where the past and present were colliding in ways that no one could have anticipated. The returnees, each with their own unique histories and expectations, were reshaping the fabric of English society, creating new opportunities and new tensions.

As the government struggled to manage the influx, nationalist groups seized on the growing unease, amplifying fears of cultural erosion and economic displacement. Protests erupted in cities across the country, with slogans like "England for the English" and "Protect Our Heritage" echoing through the streets. The returnees, many of whom had arrived with hope and optimism, found themselves facing hostility and suspicion.

For Sarah, these tensions were a reminder of the fragility of national identity. The idea of Englishness, once taken for granted, was now being questioned and redefined in real-time. The country was at a crossroads, and the path it chose would determine not just its future, but the future of all those who called it home.

As the weeks turned into months, the challenges of The Great Return became more apparent. Housing shortages led to the creation of sprawling temporary settlements on the outskirts of major cities, while the strain on public services reached breaking point. The government, under increasing pressure, implemented emergency measures to manage the crisis, but these often felt like band-aid solutions to a much deeper wound.

Sarah continued to document the unfolding story, her work taking her from the crowded streets of London to the rural villages where the impact of the return was less visible but no less profound. In every place she visited, she found people grappling with the same questions: What does it mean to be English? How do we integrate so many new people into a society that is already divided? And what kind of future are we building for the next generation?

In one particularly poignant interview, Sarah spoke with John McGuire, a union leader in the North of England who had spent his life fighting for workers' rights. John was a pragmatist, someone who understood the realities of economic hardship and social change. But even he was struggling to make sense of the new landscape.

"The returnees—they're not the problem," John said, his voice steady but weary. "The problem is that we've been ignoring these issues for years. The Great Return has just brought them to the surface. We've got to find a way to make this work, for everyone's sake. But it's going to take more than good intentions—it's going to take real, hard work and a willingness to confront the uncomfortable truths about who we are as a nation."

Sarah left the interview with a renewed sense of purpose. The story of The Great Return was not just a story of migration or identity—it was a story of a country coming to terms with itself, of people trying to find their place in a world that was changing faster than they could keep up with.

As she walked through the streets of London, Sarah couldn't

shake the feeling that she was witnessing the beginning of something monumental. The Great Return was not just a moment in history—it was the genesis of a new era, one that would redefine England and its people for generations to come.

And as she prepared to write her next article, Sarah knew that the questions she was grappling with were the same questions that would shape the future of the nation. What does it mean to belong? How do we reconcile the past with the present? And what kind of country do we want to be?

The answers were still unclear, but one thing was certain: England was at a turning point, and the choices made in the coming days, months, and years would determine its path forward.

2

TENSIONS RISING

The first few months after the GMU's decree passed in a haze of uncertainty and confusion. While some in England tried to continue their lives as though nothing had changed, the reality of The Great Return loomed larger with each passing day. The government, still struggling to manage the influx, was besieged by logistical nightmares and growing unrest among its citizens. The promise of a seamless integration had proven to be an illusion, and the cracks in the system were beginning to show.

In the corridors of power, Prime Minister James Harper found himself beset by crises on all sides. The initial optimism that had accompanied the GMU's announcement—fuelled by dreams of a rejuvenated England filled with its dispersed descendants—had given way to a sobering reality. The country was woefully unprepared to absorb the millions of returnees, and the strain on resources was becoming untenable.

Harper's government had instituted emergency measures in

an attempt to manage the situation: expanding housing projects, increasing funding for public services, and attempting to fast-track integration programs. But for every step forward, there seemed to be two steps back. The bureaucratic machine, already sluggish under the weight of austerity and years of neglect, was buckling under the pressure.

In the media, the narrative was split. Some outlets portrayed The Great Return as a noble effort to correct historical wrongs—a way for England to reclaim its people and its identity. Others, however, focused on the growing tensions and the palpable fear spreading through communities. Stories of overcrowded schools, overburdened hospitals, and rising crime rates filled the airwaves, feeding into the anxieties of a population already on edge.

For Sarah James, the escalating tensions were both a professional boon and a personal burden. Her journalism was in high demand, and her work documenting the stories of returnees and natives alike was gaining widespread attention. But the deeper she delved into the unfolding crisis, the more she struggled with her own sense of identity and belonging.

One afternoon, as she prepared for yet another interview, Sarah received a call from her editor. "We need you to cover the protests in Birmingham," he said, his voice tinged with urgency. "It's getting ugly down there, and we need someone on the ground who can make sense of it."

Sarah hesitated. She had covered protests before, but this felt different. The anger and fear that had been simmering beneath the surface for months were starting to boil over, and the situation was becoming volatile. But she knew she couldn't back down. This was the story of her lifetime, and she had to be there to capture it.

When she arrived in Birmingham, the city was a tinderbox. The streets were filled with demonstrators, their faces twisted with anger and frustration. On one side, nationalist groups had gathered to voice their opposition to the influx of returnees, waving signs with slogans like "Protect Our Heritage" and "England for the English." On the other side, counter-protesters, many of them returnees or their supporters, stood defiantly, chanting slogans of unity and inclusion.

The police, caught in the middle, were struggling to keep the two sides apart. The air was thick with tension, and it was clear that it wouldn't take much to spark violence. Sarah moved cautiously through the crowd, her press badge visible, but it offered little protection in an atmosphere so charged with emotion.

She managed to find a vantage point near the action, where she could observe both sides. The chants from the nationalist groups grew louder, more aggressive, as they pressed against the police barricades. In the midst of the crowd, she spotted a familiar face—Jenny Howard, standing with a group of returnees who had come to show their support for the counter-protesters.

Jenny's presence surprised Sarah. She had known the woman to be thoughtful, even cautious, in her approach to the tensions surrounding The Great Return. But here she was, in the thick of the confrontation, her face set with determination. It was a stark reminder of how deeply the crisis was affecting everyone, forcing even those who had tried to remain above the fray to take sides.

Sarah approached Jenny, keeping her voice low to avoid drawing too much attention. "Jenny, what are you doing here?"

Jenny turned to her, her expression softening slightly. "I couldn't stay away. This is too important. We can't let fear and hate define us. If we don't stand up for each other now, then what kind of future are we building?"

Before Sarah could respond, a sudden surge from the crowd pushed the police line back, and chaos erupted. The two sides clashed, fists flying, and the air filled with the sound of shouts and the sharp crack of police batons. Sarah's instinct took over, and she moved quickly to the edge of the melee, her camera snapping pictures as she documented the violence unfolding before her eyes.

Jenny, too, was caught in the chaos. A group of nationalists spotted her and began hurling insults, their anger palpable. They saw her as a symbol of everything they were fighting against—a wealthy returnee with no claim to the England they wanted to preserve. For a moment, it looked as though the confrontation would turn physical, but Jenny held her ground, refusing to be intimidated.

Finally, the police managed to regain control, forcing the two groups apart and dispersing the crowd. But the damage had been done. The city had witnessed a level of violence it hadn't seen in years, and the divisions in English society had been laid bare for all to see.

As the crowd thinned, Sarah found Jenny again, her face flushed but unbowed. "That was brave," Sarah said, her voice tinged with admiration. "But also dangerous. You could have been seriously hurt."

Jenny shrugged, her eyes still blazing with determination. "I can't just sit back and watch this happen, Sarah. We have to do something. We have to show people that there's another way, that we can find a way to live together."

Sarah nodded, understanding the weight of Jenny's words. The Great Return was not just a test of logistics or governance—it was a test of England's soul. The country was being forced to confront its own identity, its own history, in ways that were uncomfortable and often painful.

In the aftermath of the Birmingham protests, the government's response was swift but controversial. Prime Minister Harper condemned the violence, but his call for "law and order" did little to address the underlying issues that had led to the confrontation. Critics accused him of ignoring the real concerns of both sides, of failing to provide a vision for how England could move forward in the face of such deep divisions.

The protests in Birmingham were not an isolated incident. Across the country, similar scenes were playing out in cities and towns, as communities struggled to adapt to the realities of The Great Return. In Manchester, schools were overwhelmed by the sudden influx of new students, most of which had foreign accents, also many had never experienced the British education system. In rural areas, tensions simmered as long-time residents clashed with returnees over scarce resources and cultural differences, with varying perspectives of what it meant to be English. How could you trust someone who didn't know or love football, as in 'soccer'?

The media, too, played a significant role in shaping public perception of the crisis. Sensationalist headlines stoked fears of an "invasion," while more measured reports highlighted the struggles and triumphs of returnees trying to build new lives in their ancestral homeland. The narrative was far from unified, reflecting the broader uncertainties and conflicts within society.

As the situation grew more complex, Sarah found herself drawn deeper into the stories she was covering. She spent time with families who had returned to England with nothing but a few possessions and a sense of hope, only to find themselves living in crowded, makeshift housing with little access to the opportunities they needed to survive. She interviewed community leaders trying to bridge the gap between returnees and native-born citizens, their efforts often met with resistance and skepticism.

One of the most poignant stories Sarah encountered was that of Alex Turner, a returnee from South Africa who had been a minority union leader there, fighting against legislated affirmative action policies that disadvantaged white male workers. Now in England, Alex found himself in a country grappling with its own forms of division and inequality.

"I thought I was leaving one set of problems behind," Alex told Sarah during their interview. "But it turns out the same issues are here, just in different forms. People are scared, and when they're scared, they look for someone to blame. I've seen it before, and I'm seeing it again now."

Alex's experience highlighted the broader challenges of The Great Return. It wasn't just about moving people from one place to another—it was about integrating them into a society that was itself struggling with questions of identity and belonging. The returnees brought with them their own histories, their own struggles, and their own expectations, which often clashed with the realities of life in modern England.

As Sarah continued her work, she began to see the outlines of a larger conflict taking shape. The Great Return was not just a policy; it was a catalyst for a broader reckoning. The divisions in English society, long ignored or papered over, were now being exposed in ways that could no longer be ignored.

The question on everyone's mind was whether England could survive this reckoning. Could the country find a way to integrate over 200 million returnees while also addressing the legitimate concerns of its native-born citizens? Or would the tensions and divisions prove too great, leading to a fracturing of society that would be impossible to repair? England's native-born citizens who were now in the minority of three to one were clearly going to have to accept change, how would that be managed? What would the gains and pains be, and for who?

As Sarah looked out over the city from her flat that evening, she couldn't shake the feeling that the future of England was hanging in the balance. The choices made in the coming days, weeks, and months would determine not just the outcome of The Great Return, but the very identity of the nation itself.

For now, all she could do was continue to document the stories of those caught up in the maelstrom, hoping that by shining a light on their experiences, she might help guide the country toward a future where everyone could find a place to belong.

3

Fault Lines

The crisis in England continued to escalate as the government's attempts to manage The Great Return faltered. The initial excitement and hope that had accompanied the announcement were quickly overshadowed by the harsh realities of integrating millions of returnees into a country already grappling with its own issues. The previous political differences, and social cracks in society, momentarily hidden beneath the tumultuous surface of initial remigrations, were now spewing again, widening into fault lines that threatened to tear the nation apart.

In London, the atmosphere was tense. The city, always a melting pot of cultures and identities, was now struggling under the weight of the influx. The government's emergency measures had provided some relief, but they were little more than temporary fixes to a problem that required deep, systemic change.

Sarah James continued her work as a journalist, documenting the unfolding story. The more she reported, the more she realised that The Great Return was exposing not just the divisions between returnees and native-born citizens, but also the deeper inequalities that had long plagued English society. The returnees were not just a new demographic—they were a catalyst for revealing the fault lines that had been ignored for too long.

One morning, as Sarah was preparing for another day of interviews, she received a call from her editor. "I've got something for you," he said, his voice carrying a hint of urgency. "There's a new housing development in Greater London, one of the government's solutions to the overcrowding. But it's turning into a flashpoint. I want you to go down there and see what's going on."

The housing development, known as New Haven, had been built on the outskirts of the city to accommodate the growing number of returnees. It was intended to be a model of modern urban planning—affordable, sustainable, and designed to foster a sense of community. But from the moment Sarah arrived, it was clear that New Haven was far from the utopia it was meant to be.

The streets were lined with identical, hastily constructed buildings, their facades already showing signs of wear. The people who lived there—a mix of returnees and native-born citizens—were frustrated and disillusioned. The promises of a better life had given way to the reality of overcrowding, limited resources, and a sense of isolation from the rest of the city.

As Sarah walked through the development, she struck up a conversation with Angie Wilson, a returnee from Kansas who had moved to New Haven with her family. Angie's story was one of many Sarah had heard—a tale of great pain, but clinging to a hope that was repeatedly lashed at by the harsh realities of integration.

"We were forced to come here, but we remained hopeful, we thought it would be a good, fresh start," Angie said, her voice tinged with frustration. "But we've just been pushed to the margins. The schools are overcrowded, the public services are stretched to the limit, and there's this feeling that we're not really welcome here. Like, we were happy in Kansas."

Sarah listened, sensing the undercurrent of tension in Angie's words. The returnees had been remigrated to England with the expectation from the government that they would be embraced as part of the nation's identity, but instead, they were finding themselves caught in a liminal space—neither fully accepted nor entirely rejected.

As they continued to talk, Sarah learned more about the challenges facing the residents of New Haven. The housing development, far from fostering community, had become a microcosm of the broader societal divisions. The returnees, many of whom were struggling to adapt to life in England, were clashing with native-born citizens who felt that their own needs were being ignored in favour of accommodating the newcomers.

One of the most contentious issues was employment. Many of the returnees were highly skilled, but their qualifications were not always recognised in England. This had led to frustration and resentment as they found themselves unable to secure jobs that matched their skills. At the same time, native-born citizens, already facing economic hardships, saw the returnees as competition for the limited opportunities available.

Sarah met with John McGuire again, the union leader she had interviewed before. He had been working with the residents of New Haven to address their concerns, but even he admitted that the situation was becoming increasingly difficult to manage.

"The problem is that we're dealing with multiple crises at once," John explained. "The returnees are struggling to find their place in a society that's already fractured, and the native-born citizens feel like they're being pushed aside. It's a powder keg, and if we're not careful, it's going to explode."

John's words were prophetic. As the weeks passed, tensions in New Haven continued to rise. The local council, overwhelmed by the demands of the development, was unable to provide adequate support. Protests broke out, with residents demanding better services and more support from the government. These protests quickly turned into clashes between returnees and native-born citizens, each group blaming the other for their difficulties.

The media coverage of the clashes only served to inflame tensions further. Sensationalist headlines painted the returnees as invaders, while more sympathetic outlets highlighted the struggles of those who were simply trying to build a new life in their ancestral homeland. The narrative was polarised, reflecting the broader divisions in English society.

Amidst this turmoil, Sarah found herself increasingly conflicted. As a journalist, her role was to report the truth, but the truth was complicated. The returnees were not a monolithic group, and neither were the native-born citizens. There were stories of cooperation and understanding, just as there were stories of conflict and division.

One evening, as Sarah sat in her flat, reviewing her notes from the day, she received an unexpected call from The Fixer. The mysterious figure had become something of an enigma in Sarah's life—a source of information and insight, but also someone whose motives were never entirely clear.

"I hear you've been spending time in New Haven," The Fixer said, their voice as calm and measured as ever.

"Yes," Sarah replied, unsure of where the conversation was

headed. "It's a mess down there. People are angry, scared. It feels like the whole thing is about to unravel."

"It might," The Fixer agreed. "But it's important to remember that this isn't just about New Haven. The situation there is a symptom of a much larger problem. The returnees are the catalyst, but the underlying issues have been there for a long time. If you want to understand what's really going on, you need to look beyond the immediate conflict."

Sarah frowned, not entirely sure what The Fixer was getting at. "What do you mean?"

"There are forces at work here that go beyond what you're seeing on the surface," The Fixer continued. "The Consortium, for one. They're not just interested in the returnees—they're interested in using the chaos to their advantage. They thrive on division, on instability. The more fractured England becomes, the more power they can consolidate."

The mention of The Consortium sent a chill down Sarah's spine. She had heard whispers about the shadowy organisation, but she had never been able to find concrete evidence of their involvement. Now, it seemed, they were becoming more brazen in their efforts to manipulate the situation.

"What are they trying to do?" Sarah asked, her voice low.

"Control," The Fixer replied simply. "They want to control

the narrative, control the outcome. If they can push England to the brink, they can reshape it in their image. But that doesn't have to happen. There are still people fighting for a different future, people who believe that England can come through this stronger, more united. You have a role to play in that, Sarah."

The call ended abruptly, leaving Sarah with more questions than answers. The idea that The Great Return was being manipulated by outside forces was both alarming and unsurprising. The crisis was too large, too complex, for there not to be those who sought to exploit it for their own gain.

As Sarah sat back in her chair, her mind racing, she knew that her work had taken on a new urgency. It was no longer just about documenting the stories of those caught up in The Great Return—it was about uncovering the truth behind the crisis, about shining a light on the forces that were shaping England's future.

The next day, Sarah returned to New Haven with renewed determination. She sought out more voices, digging deeper into the stories of the people living there. She spoke with returnees who had been doctors, engineers, and teachers in their former lives, now reduced to taking whatever work they could find. She interviewed native-born citizens who felt betrayed by a government that seemed more concerned with accommodating newcomers than with addressing their needs.

And she began to piece together a picture of a country at a crossroads. The Great Return was not just a challenge—it was an opportunity. An opportunity to confront the inequalities and divisions that had long plagued England, to build a society that was more just, more inclusive. But it was also a test, a test of whether the country could rise to the occasion or whether it would succumb to fear and division.

As the days turned into weeks, Sarah's work began to gain attention. Her articles were shared widely, sparking debates and discussions across the country. She became a voice for those who felt unheard, a chronicler of the struggles and triumphs of a nation in transition.

But even as she sought to shed light on the truth, Sarah knew that the battle for England's future was far from over. The fault lines that had been exposed were deep, and the forces working to widen them were powerful. The Consortium, the nationalist groups, the economic disparities—they were all part of a larger web of challenges that would take years, if not decades, to untangle.

And yet, amidst the uncertainty, there was also hope. The returnees, for all their struggles, were resilient. Their remigration to England came with messages of The Great Return being about creating a better life, without specifying who the message was for specifically, or how this new great life would happen. But many were determined to build it, despite the obstacles in their way. The native-born citizens, too, were not monolithic in their views. There were those who saw the returnees not as threats, but as potential allies in the fight for a better future.

As Sarah continued her work, she realised that the story of The Great Return was not just a story of division—it was also a story of possibility. The possibility of a new England, one that was stronger, more inclusive, and more united than before. But to reach that future, the country would have to confront its past, its present, and the forces that sought to shape its destiny.

The fault lines were there, but so too were the bridges that could be built across them. And it was up to the people of England, both returnees and native-born, to decide which path they would take.

Paul Weatherdon - The Great Return - Emigrants, come home!

4

THE UNDERBELLY

As the turmoil of The Great Return continued to spread across England, it became clear that the crisis was not just about managing the influx of people; it was about grappling with the darker aspects of society that had been hidden for too long. Beneath the surface of public discourse, a shadowy network of opportunists, criminals, and conspirators was emerging, seeking to exploit the chaos for their own gain. These were the forces that Sarah James had been warned about by The Fixer, and as she dug deeper into the story, she began to uncover the underbelly of England's transformation.

In London, the government was struggling to maintain control. The city, which had always prided itself on its diversity and resilience, was now teetering on the edge. The returnees, who had come with hopes of rebuilding their lives in the land of their ancestors, were finding themselves caught in a web of corruption and exploitation. The housing crisis, already dire, had opened the door for unscrupulous landlords and developers to take advantage of the most vulnerable.

Sarah's investigation into the housing developments like New Haven revealed a disturbing pattern. The government contracts to build and manage these new communities had been awarded to companies with dubious backgrounds, many of them with ties to The Consortium. These companies had cut corners, using substandard materials and underpaying workers, all while pocketing enormous profits. The result was a landscape of crumbling buildings and broken promises, with the returnees paying the price.

One of Sarah's contacts, a whistleblower within the Department of Housing, provided her with documents that exposed the extent of the corruption. The contracts had been signed off by high-ranking officials, many of whom had received substantial kickbacks in return. The implications were staggering—this was not just about mismanagement, it was about systemic corruption that reached the highest levels of government.

With this information in hand, Sarah knew she was sitting on a story that could shake the very foundations of the government. But she also knew that exposing it would put her in serious danger. The Consortium, already aware of her investigations, would stop at nothing to protect its interests. She needed to be careful, to gather more evidence and to find allies who could help her bring the truth to light.

One such ally was Victoria Langley, a rising star in the political arena who had made a name for herself as a fierce advocate for transparency and reform. Langley had been one of the few voices in Parliament to speak out against the way The Great Return was being handled, and she had gained a following among both returnees and native-born citizens who were frustrated with the government's response.

Sarah arranged to meet with Langley at her office in Westminster. As she walked through the grand corridors of power, she couldn't help but feel a sense of unease. The stakes were higher than ever, and she knew that what she was about to reveal could change the course of her life—and the future of the country.

Langley greeted her with a firm handshake and led her into a small, private meeting room. The MP was a striking figure, with a sharp intellect and a presence that commanded attention. Sarah wasted no time in laying out what she had discovered, showing Langley the documents and explaining the connections she had uncovered between the housing developments, The Consortium, and the government.

Langley listened intently, her expression growing more serious as Sarah spoke. When Sarah finished, there was a long moment of silence as Langley processed the information.

"This is explosive," Langley finally said, her voice measured. "If what you're saying is true, this could bring down the government. But it also puts you—and anyone involved—at great risk. The people behind this won't hesitate to protect themselves."

"I know," Sarah replied, her voice steady despite the fear gnawing at her. "But the truth needs to come out. People need to know what's really happening, and those responsible need to be held accountable."

Langley nodded, her gaze intense. "You're right. But we need to be smart about this. We can't just go public without a plan. We need to gather more evidence, build a case that's airtight. And we need to be prepared for the fallout."

The two women spent the next few hours strategising, discussing how they could gather more evidence and who they could trust to help them. Langley agreed to use her political connections to quietly investigate the officials involved, while Sarah would continue her work on the ground, digging deeper into the housing crisis and The Consortium's influence.

As Sarah left the meeting, she felt a mix of resolve and anxiety. She had taken the first step in what would likely be a dangerous journey, but she knew it was the right thing to do. The people of England deserved better than what they were getting, and she was determined to fight for justice, no matter the cost.

Back in the heart of London, the impact of the corruption was becoming more visible. The temporary settlements on the outskirts of the city, where many returnees had been forced to live, were turning into slums. Basic services were scarce, and the conditions were deteriorating rapidly. The promises of opportunity and integration had given way to a grim reality of poverty and neglect.

Sarah visited one of these settlements, accompanied by a local activist named Mary Smith, who had been working tirelessly to support the returnees. Mary was a fierce advocate for human rights, and she had seen firsthand the devastating impact of the government's failures.

As they walked through the settlement, Sarah was struck by the harshness of life there. Children played in the dirt, their faces etched with a weariness far beyond their years. Families lived in makeshift shelters, cobbled together from whatever materials they could find. The air was thick with despair, and the tension was palpable.

"This is what happens when greed and corruption take precedence over people," Mary said bitterly as they watched a group of women huddled around a small fire, cooking what little food they had. "These people, forced to come here, are filled with hope from all the sponsored messaging, but that hope is being destroyed by those who only care about lining their pockets."

Sarah nodded, feeling a surge of anger and frustration. The stories she had heard, the images she had captured, all pointed to a systemic failure that went beyond mere incompetence. It was a failure of ethics, of humanity, and it was tearing the fabric of the nation apart, in ways past generations could never have imagined.

They continued through the settlement, speaking with residents who shared their stories of broken promises and dashed hopes. Many had been professionals in their former countries—doctors, teachers, engineers—but here, they were reduced to begging for work, struggling just to survive.

One man, Simon, had been a civil engineer in Texas. He had been remigrated to England with his family, expecting that his skills would be in demand. But after months of searching, he had found only rejection and prejudice.

"They look at me and see a foreigner," Simon said, his voice heavy with resignation. "They don't care that I have the skills to help rebuild this country. All they see is someone who doesn't belong. And now, we're trapped here, forgotten by the very government that brought us back."

Sarah's heart ached as she listened to Simon's story, one of many she had heard that day. It was a reminder of the human cost of the corruption and exploitation she was investigating. These were real people, with real lives and real dreams, and they were being crushed by a system that was supposed to receive them in ways that would build people's spirit, not tear it apart.

As the sun began to set, Sarah and Mary made their way back to the edge of the settlement. The day had been exhausting, both physically and emotionally, but Sarah knew that her work was far from over. The more she uncovered, the more determined she became to expose the truth and hold those responsible accountable.

But as she prepared to leave, she couldn't shake the feeling that she was being watched. The settlement, once bustling with activity, had grown quiet, and the shadows seemed to stretch longer than they should. Sarah glanced around, her senses on high alert, but saw nothing out of the ordinary.

"Are you okay?" Mary asked, noticing Sarah's unease.

"Yeah," Sarah replied, forcing a smile. "Just tired, I guess."

But as they drove away from the settlement, the feeling of being watched lingered. Sarah knew that she was treading dangerous ground, and the stakes were getting higher with each passing day. The forces she was up against were powerful, and they would not hesitate to silence anyone who threatened their interests.

That night, as Sarah sat in her flat, reviewing her notes and photos, she received another call from The Fixer.

"You were at the settlement today," The Fixer said, their

voice as calm and measured as ever. "Be careful, Sarah. You're drawing attention, and not the good kind."

"I know," Sarah replied, trying to keep her voice steady. "But I can't stop now. There's too much at stake."

"I understand," The Fixer said. "But you need to be smart about this. The people you're up against won't hesitate to do whatever it takes to protect themselves. Watch your back, and don't trust anyone too easily. You're on the right path, but it's a dangerous one."

The call ended as abruptly as it had begun, leaving Sarah with a sense of foreboding. She was in deep now, backing out was not an option. The investigation had taken on a life of its own, and Sarah knew that she was closing in on something big—something that could change everything.

But with each step forward, the risks grew greater. The Consortium, the corrupt officials, the shadowy figures operating in the underbelly of society—they were all watching, waiting for the right moment to strike. And Sarah knew that if she wasn't careful, she could become their next target.

As she lay in bed that night, sleep eluded her. Her mind was a whirlwind of thoughts, of plans, of fears. The underbelly of England's transformation was darker and more dangerous than she had ever imagined, and she was about to plunge headfirst into it.

But despite the fear, there was also a steely resolve. Sarah had always believed in the power of truth, in the importance of holding those in power accountable. And now, more than ever, she was determined to see this through, no matter the cost.

England was at a crossroads, and the choices made in the coming days would determine its future. Sarah was ready to do her part, to shine a light on the darkness and fight for a future where justice and integrity prevailed.

But first, she would need to survive the journey.

Paul Weatherdon - The Great Return - Emigrants, come home!

5

THE SHIFTING SANDS

The growing tension across England was palpable, as the fabric of society stretched and strained under the weight of The Great Return. The crisis was no longer just about logistics or resources; it had become a profound challenge to the very identity of the nation. As just over 200 million people with primarily English DNA from around the world, returned to a country with a native-born, English DNA population of just 35 million people, they brought with them a complex mix of cultures, experiences, and expectations. This was not a simple homecoming—it was a collision of past and present, of history and the modern world.

In cities and towns across England, the presence of the returnees was impossible to ignore. The government's attempts to manage the influx had been uneven at best, and the consequences were playing out in real-time. While some returnees had managed to integrate relatively smoothly, finding jobs and homes, others were struggling to adapt to a country that, while technically their homeland, felt foreign and unwelcoming.

Sarah James was deep into her investigation, and the more she uncovered, the more complex the situation became. Her focus had shifted slightly, moving from the immediate logistical challenges of The Great Return to the underlying social and cultural tensions that were emerging. The stories she was documenting were not just about people returning to England—they were about the clash of identities, the redefinition of what it meant to be English in the 21st century.

One such story was that of Michael Fraser, a returnee from New Zealand. Michael's family had left England generations ago, seeking a new life on the other side of the world. He had grown up with stories of old England, but they had always seemed distant, almost mythical. When The Great Return was announced, Michael, took it as an opportunity to reconnect with his ancestral roots.

Michael had arrived in London with his wife, Claire, and their two young children. They had been full of hope, excited to start a new chapter in their lives. But the reality of life in England was far from what they had imagined. Despite his qualifications and experience as a civil engineer, Michael struggled to find work. The housing situation was equally challenging; the family ended up in one of the government's new developments, which was already overcrowded, under-resourced and its boundaries blending into a sprawling slum. When Sarah met Michael for an interview, he was clearly frustrated. "We coloured our remigration with a hope to reconnect with our roots, to give our children the chance to grow up in the country their ancestors came from. But it feels like we've been thrown into a situation that no one was prepared for. The England I'd heard about from my grandparents doesn't seem to exist anymore."

Claire, who had been listening quietly, nodded in agreement. "We knew it wouldn't be easy, but we didn't expect it to be this hard. It's not just about finding a job or a place to live—it's about feeling like we belong. And right now, I'm not sure we do."

Sarah could sense the disillusionment in their voices, a sentiment that was becoming increasingly common among the returnees she had spoken to. The idealised vision of England that many had carried with them was being confronted by the harsh realities of a country struggling with its own identity crisis.

As Sarah continued her work, she began to notice a pattern. The returnees who were struggling the most were often those who had come from countries where the English diaspora had integrated into the local culture over generations—places like Australia, Canada, and New Zealand. These returnees, while technically English by blood, had grown up in environments where their identity was shaped by a mix of influences, making their transition to life in modern England more difficult.

In contrast, returnees from countries with more recent English connections, such as South Africa or Zimbabwe, often found it easier to adapt, particularly if they had maintained strong ties to English culture. But even for them, the challenges were significant. The England they had returned to was not the England their ancestors had left behind, and the differences were stark.

One of the most poignant stories Sarah encountered was that of Alexandra "Alex" Cartwright, a returnee from Zimbabwe. Alex's family had been part of the British colonial presence in Southern Africa for generations, and she had grown up in a community that still identified strongly with English traditions and culture. When The Great Return was announced, Alex saw her forced remigration positively, as a chance to reconnect with her heritage and to escape the political and economic instability of Zimbabwe.

But life in England was not what Alex had expected. Despite her English roots, she found herself feeling out of place, caught between two worlds. The England of her grandparents' stories, with its quaint villages and sense of community, was hard to find in the bustling, modern country she now called home.

"I always felt English, even when I was living in Zimbabwe," Alex told Sarah during their interview. "But now that I'm here, I realise that my idea of England was more about the past than the present. The country has changed, and I'm struggling to find my place in it."

Alex had been a teacher in Zimbabwe, but in England, she found it difficult to get her qualifications recognised. The bureaucracy was overwhelming, and the job market was competitive. She eventually found work as a teaching assistant, but it was a far cry from the career she had envisioned for herself.

"It's not just about the job," Alex explained. "It's about feeling like I'm contributing, like I'm part of something. But right now, I feel like I'm just going through the motions, trying to survive in a place that doesn't quite feel like home."

Sarah listened, recognising the echoes of similar sentiments she had heard from other returnees. The idea of "coming home" was complicated by the reality that home was not just a place—it was a feeling, a sense of belonging that was not easily attained.

As Sarah delved deeper into these stories, she began to see how The Great Return was forcing England to confront its own history in ways that were both challenging and uncomfortable. The returnees were not just bringing themselves—they were bringing the legacies of empire, migration, and cultural exchange that had shaped their identities. And these legacies were now clashing with the modern English culture. Who puts vinegar on their crisps?

In addition to her interviews with returnees, Sarah also began to explore the perspectives of native-born citizens who were grappling with the changes in their communities. In the town of Norwich, she met George Bennett, a retired factory worker who had lived in the same house for over fifty years. George's ancestors had been working-class English, and he had always taken pride in his roots.

But the arrival of returnees in Norwich had unsettled George. The town, once a close-knit community where everyone knew each other, was now a place of rapid change. New faces, new accents, new customs—these were all things that George found difficult to accept.

"It's not that I don't want them here," George said, his voice laced with a mix of frustration and confusion. "But it feels like everything's changing too fast. The England I grew up in is disappearing, and I'm not sure what's replacing it."

George's concerns were echoed by others in the town, many of whom were struggling to reconcile their pride in their English heritage with the realities of a changing society. For them, The Great Return was not just about the returnees—it was about what it meant for the future of their country, for their sense of identity, and the nation's role in the new world-order.

Sarah could see that the tensions were not just about economics or resources—they were about deeper, more existential questions. What did it mean to be English in a world where the past was colliding with the present? How could a nation that had built its identity on the idea of empire and global influence now reconcile itself with the return of its diaspora?

These were questions that had no easy answers, but they were questions that England would have to face if it was to move forward. The returnees, with their diverse backgrounds and experiences, were both a challenge and an opportunity. They were a reminder that England's history was not just its own—it was a shared history, a global history, and one that could not be easily compartmentalised.

As Sarah continued her investigation, she also kept a close eye on the activities of The Consortium. The shadowy organisation had remained largely in the background, but its influence was becoming increasingly apparent. The housing developments, the corruption, the exploitation of returnees—these were all symptoms of a larger problem, one that Sarah was determined to expose.

But she knew that the path ahead was fraught with danger. The Consortium was powerful, and its reach extended into the highest levels of government and business. Sarah's investigation had already attracted attention, and she was acutely aware that she was being watched.

Despite the risks, Sarah pressed on. She knew that the story of The Great Return was more than just a human interest piece—it was a story about the future of England, about the choices that would define the nation for generations to come. The shifting sands of identity, history, and power were all at play, and Sarah was determined to document every moment of it. As the country grappled with the challenges of integration, belonging, and justice, Sarah's work took on new urgency. The returnees, the native-born citizens, the shadowy forces behind the scenes—they were all part of a larger narrative, one that was still unfolding.

And as Sarah prepared for the next stage of her investigation, she knew that the stakes had never been higher. England was changing, and the choices made in the coming days, weeks, and months would determine the kind of country it would become.

But one thing was certain: The Great Return was not just a moment in time—it was a turning point, a moment of reckoning that would shape the future of England and its people for years to come.

6

THE GATHERING STORM

As England continued to grapple with the implications of The Great Return, the storm clouds of unrest were gathering, both figuratively and literally. The social and economic pressures were mounting, and the divisions within the country were becoming more pronounced. The government, already struggling to manage the logistical challenges of integrating hundreds of millions of returnees, now faced a new crisis: the threat of widespread civil unrest. With native-born citizens in a severe minority, they'd fight with their backs to the corner like a trapped wild animal, ignoring the knowledge they'd be labelled as far-right by the government and arrested as criminals, in a superb piece of government communications controlling the narrative and law.

Sarah James was at the forefront of reporting on these developments, her work increasingly focused on the growing tensions between the returnees and the native-born citizens. The uneasy coexistence that had characterised the early days of The Great Return was beginning to fracture, and the country was teetering on the edge of a full-blown crisis.

In the industrial city of Birmingham, where Sarah had covered earlier protests, the situation had reached a boiling point. The city, historically a hub of working-class life and industry, was now one of the epicentres of the unrest. The returnees, many of whom had found themselves living in overcrowded and underfunded housing developments, were increasingly at odds with the long-time residents who felt they were being displaced in their own city.

The economic disparities that had been simmering beneath the surface for years were now erupting into open conflict. Factories that had once provided steady employment for the city's residents had closed or downsized, leaving many without work. The arrival of the returnees, many of whom were competing for the same scarce jobs, had only exacerbated the sense of insecurity and resentment.

Sarah arrived in Birmingham on a dreary, rain-soaked day, the grey skies reflecting the mood of the city. The streets were lined with boarded-up shops and abandoned buildings, a stark reminder of the economic decline that had plagued the area for years. As she made her way to the city centre, she could see groups of people gathered in small knots, their faces grim and their voices low.

She was there to cover a rally organised by the local branch of the National Unity Front (NUF), a nationalist group that had gained significant traction in the wake of The Great Return. The NUF had positioned itself as the voice of "real" English people, those who had lived in the country for generations and who now felt that their way of life was under threat.

The rally was being held in Victoria Square, a central location that had once been a symbol of the city's prosperity. Now, it was the site of angry speeches and nationalist rhetoric, with NUF leaders calling for the government to "put England first" and to stop the "invasion" of returnees.

Sarah moved through the crowd, her camera at the ready, capturing the faces of the people who had come to support the NUF. There were older men and women, their expressions hardened by years of economic struggle, standing alongside younger men, some of whom wore the symbols of far-right groups. The mood was tense, and there was an undercurrent of violence in the air.

As she listened to the speeches, Sarah felt a deep unease. The rhetoric was inflammatory, filled with references to "defending English culture" and "taking back our country." It was the language of division, of exclusion, and it was being met with cheers and applause from the crowd.

But what concerned Sarah even more was the presence of returnees in the crowd—people who had come to England hoping to reconnect with their roots, only to find themselves alienated and drawn to the NUF's message of nationalism and belonging. She spoke to one such returnee, Henry Thompson, who had returned to England from Canada with his wife and children.

Henry's family had left England during the post-war years, seeking a better life in North America. When The Great Return was announced, Henry saw it as an opportunity to reconnect with his heritage and to give his children the chance to grow up in the country of their ancestors. But the reality of life in England had been a harsh awakening.

"We thought we'd be welcomed home," Henry said, his voice tinged with bitterness. "But instead, we've been treated like strangers, like we don't belong here. The jobs we were promised don't exist, the housing is a joke, and the government doesn't seem to care. The NUF—they're the only ones who are speaking up for people like us."

Sarah was struck by the depth of Henry's disillusionment. The NUF's message was resonating not just with native-born citizens, but with returnees who felt betrayed by the government and by the idealised vision of England they had carried with them.

As the rally continued, Sarah's attention was drawn to a confrontation at the edge of the square. A group of NUF supporters had surrounded a small group of counter-protesters, mostly young returnees who had come to voice their opposition to the NUF's message. The situation was escalating quickly, with shouts and insults being exchanged.

Sarah moved closer, her heart pounding as she anticipated the violence that seemed inevitable. The police, who had been present at the rally in small numbers, were moving in to try to defuse the situation, but it was clear they were outnumbered.

Suddenly, a scuffle broke out, and the square erupted into chaos. Sarah found herself in the middle of it, her camera clicking furiously as she documented the violence unfolding around her. She could see the fear and anger on the faces of the protesters, the desperation of people who felt they had no other way to be heard.

Amidst the chaos, Sarah caught sight of a young woman—Emily Carter—who had been knocked to the ground. Emily was a returnee from Australia, and she had been active in organising efforts to support other returnees in Birmingham. She was well-spoken and passionate, but she was no match for the force of the angry crowd around her.

Without thinking, Sarah rushed forward to help Emily, pulling her out of the fray and into a nearby alley. They both leaned against the wall, breathing heavily, the sounds of the riot still echoing in the square behind them.

"Thank you," Emily gasped, her face pale and streaked with dirt.

"Don't mention it," Sarah replied, trying to catch her breath. "Are you okay?"

"I think so," Emily said, wincing as she touched a bruise on her arm. "But this is getting out of control. This isn't what I had hoped for."

"What did you hope for?" Sarah asked, genuinely curious.

Emily hesitated, her eyes reflecting a mix of confusion and determination. "I hoped to be part of something bigger than myself. Because I believed that England could be a place where people like me could find a home, where we could contribute to something meaningful. But now... now I'm not so sure."

Sarah nodded, understanding all too well the disillusionment that Emily was feeling. The promise of The Great Return had been one of a united England, of reconnecting with roots and building a new future. But the reality was turning out to be far more complicated, and far more dangerous.

As they made their way out of the alley and away from the chaos of the square, Sarah knew that the story she was covering was about more than just a political crisis. It was about the soul of a nation, about the choices that would define the future of England and its people.

Back in London, the government was scrambling to respond to the growing unrest. Prime Minister James Harper had called for an emergency meeting of his cabinet, seeking to address the escalating violence and the deepening divisions in the country. But the challenges were overwhelming, and the solutions were elusive.

In the days following the Birmingham rally, similar incidents erupted in other cities across the country. The NUF was capitalising on the anger and fear that had taken hold, organising rallies and spreading its message of nationalism and exclusion. The returnees, who had come to England with hopes of building new lives, were increasingly caught in the crossfire.

Sarah continued to document these developments, her articles gaining widespread attention as they captured the growing sense of crisis in the country. But with each story she published, she also felt the weight of the responsibility she carried. The truth needed to be told, but she knew that the more she exposed, the more she put herself at risk.

The Fixer had warned her to be careful, and the events in Birmingham had only reinforced the dangers she faced. The Consortium was still in the shadows, pulling strings and manipulating events to serve its own agenda. And as the country continued to unravel, Sarah knew that the forces of darkness were growing stronger.

But she also knew that she couldn't stop now. The story of The Great Return was far from over, and the choices made in the coming days would determine the future of England and its people. As the storm gathered strength, Sarah was determined to stand at the forefront, documenting the truth and fighting for a future where justice and unity could prevail.

And as she prepared for her next assignment, Sarah knew that the road ahead would be difficult and dangerous. But she also knew that she had a role to play in the unfolding drama, a role that she would not abandon, no matter the cost.

7

SHADOWS IN THE STREETS

The days following the Birmingham rally were marked by an uneasy calm, the kind that precedes a storm. Across England, the tensions were palpable, simmering just below the surface as the nation struggled to come to terms with the reality of The Great Return. In cities large and small, the divisions between returnees and native-born citizens were becoming more pronounced, as each group wrestled with its own fears, frustrations, and hopes.

For Sarah James, the work was relentless. The more she uncovered, the more she realised how deep the fractures in English society ran. The returnees, with their diverse backgrounds and experiences, were finding it increasingly difficult to integrate into a country that, while technically their homeland, felt foreign and often hostile. The native-born citizens, meanwhile, were grappling with the rapid changes in their communities, fearful of losing their cultural identity and economic security.

But beneath these surface tensions lay something more insidious: the growing influence of The Consortium, the shadowy organisation that had been quietly manipulating events from behind the scenes. Sarah had long suspected that The Consortium was playing a larger role in the unfolding crisis than anyone realised, and her investigation was beginning to confirm those suspicions.

In London, the signs of unrest were everywhere. The city, always vibrant and chaotic, had taken on a new edge. The returnees, who had been forcibly remigrated to England were sold the English dream and upon that, built hopes of thriving in their new lives. In stark contrast they were now facing a reality that was far more challenging than they had anticipated. Many found themselves living in overcrowded housing developments, or the recently sprawling slums, struggling to find work, and dealing with the hostility of locals who saw them as interlopers.

One evening, as Sarah was walking through the streets of East London, she was struck by how quickly the atmosphere had changed. The neighbourhoods that had once been lively and diverse were now marked by a palpable sense of fear. Shops that had been open late were now closing their shutters early, and the streets, once filled with people from all walks of life, were now eerily quiet.

As she made her way down a narrow side street, Sarah

noticed a group of young men gathered on a corner, their faces shadowed by the dim streetlights. They were talking in low voices, their eyes scanning the street with a mix of suspicion and aggression. Sarah recognised the look—they were members of one of the nationalist groups that had been gaining traction in the wake of The Great Return.

She kept her distance, not wanting to draw attention to herself, but as she walked past, she overheard a snippet of their conversation. They were talking about a rally planned for the next day, one that would take place in the heart of the city. It was clear from their tone that they expected trouble, and that they were prepared for it.

Sarah quickened her pace, her mind racing. The prospect of another rally, especially one in central London, was alarming. The previous protests had already escalated into violence, and the idea of another confrontation, this time in the capital, filled her with dread. She knew that she had to report on it, to document what was happening, but she also knew that it would be dangerous.

The next day, Sarah made her way to the site of the rally, her camera slung over her shoulder and her press badge clearly visible. The location—a large public square near the financial district—was already filling up with people by the time she arrived. On one side were the nationalist groups, their flags and banners declaring their opposition to The Great Return and their desire to "take back England." On the other side were the counter-protesters, a mix of returnees and their supporters, holding signs that called for unity and acceptance.

The atmosphere was tense, the air thick with the anticipation of conflict. The police were out in force, their presence a stark reminder of the potential for violence. Sarah positioned herself at the edge of the square, close enough to capture the action but far enough away to avoid getting caught up in the fray.

As the rally began, the leaders of the nationalist groups took to the stage, their voices amplified by loudspeakers. Their speeches were fiery, filled with rhetoric about defending English culture and protecting the nation from the "invaders" who had returned. The crowd responded with cheers and chants, their anger palpable.

But as the speeches continued, Sarah noticed something that set her on edge. Among the nationalist crowd were several figures who didn't quite fit in—men in suits, their expressions inscrutable, who seemed more interested in observing than participating. Sarah recognised the type; these were not ordinary protesters, but operatives of some kind, likely connected to The Consortium.

She watched them closely, her camera capturing their faces, their movements. They were careful, deliberate, as if they were waiting for something. It didn't take long for Sarah to realise what it was.

A few minutes later, as one of the nationalist leaders was reaching the climax of his speech, a group of counter-protesters attempted to move closer to the stage, their chants growing louder in an effort to drown out the speaker. The police moved to block them, but it was too late. A scuffle broke out, and within moments, the square erupted into chaos.

Sarah moved quickly, her camera clicking furiously as she documented the violence unfolding before her. The nationalist groups, emboldened by the presence of their leaders, surged forward, clashing with the counter-protesters and the police. The operatives she had noticed earlier were now in the thick of it, their actions subtle but effective as they steered the crowd towards more violent confrontation.

As the situation spiralled out of control, Sarah felt a hand on her arm, pulling her back. She turned to see John McGuire, the union leader she had worked with before. His face was grim, his eyes scanning the scene with a mix of concern and anger.

"Sarah, you need to get out of here," he said urgently. "This is going to get ugly."

"I'm not leaving," Sarah replied, her voice firm. "I need to document this."

"Fine," John said, his grip tightening slightly. "But stay close to me. I don't trust what's happening here."

The two of them moved through the crowd, Sarah continuing to take photos while John kept a watchful eye on their surroundings. The violence was spreading, the police struggling to regain control as more and more people joined the fray. It was clear that this was no ordinary protest—it was something orchestrated, something designed to push the situation to the brink.

As they made their way to the edge of the square, Sarah spotted one of the operatives she had noticed earlier. He was standing near a side street, his phone to his ear, his expression cold and calculating. Without thinking, Sarah raised her camera and snapped a photo, capturing the moment before he could disappear.

The man looked up sharply, his eyes locking onto Sarah. For a moment, she felt a surge of fear—had she gone too far? But then he turned and walked away, disappearing into the crowd as if he had never been there.

Sarah lowered her camera, her heart racing. She knew that she had captured something important, something that could expose the true nature of what was happening. But she also knew that she had made herself a target. The Consortium was not an organisation that tolerated exposure, and she had just crossed a line.

Back at her flat that evening, Sarah reviewed the photos she had taken. The images were powerful, capturing the raw emotion and violence of the rally, but it was the photo of the operative that held her attention. There was something about his expression, something that hinted at the cold calculation behind the chaos.

She sent the photo to her editor, along with a detailed report of what she had witnessed. As she hit send, she knew that the coming days would be critical. The situation in England was escalating, and the forces behind it were becoming more brazen.

But Sarah also knew that she had to keep going. The truth needed to be exposed, no matter the cost. The country was on the brink, and the choices made now would determine its future.

That night, as Sarah lay in bed, she received another call from The Fixer.

"You were at the rally today," The Fixer said, their voice as calm as ever.

"Yes," Sarah replied, her voice steady. "I saw them. The operatives."

"I know," The Fixer said. "You need to be careful, Sarah. They're watching you now."

"I figured as much," Sarah said, trying to keep the fear out of her voice. "But I'm not stopping."

"Good," The Fixer said. "But remember—you're walking a dangerous path. Watch your back, and don't trust anyone."

The call ended, leaving Sarah with a sense of foreboding. The shadows were closing in, and the storm was gathering strength. But she was determined to see it through, to expose the truth and fight for a future where justice could prevail.

The streets of London were dark and quiet as she finally drifted off to sleep, the sounds of the city a distant echo. But even in her dreams, the shadows lingered, a reminder of the dangers that lay ahead.

8

FRACTURES IN THE FOUNDATION

The unrest that had been simmering across England was beginning to boil over, and the fractures in the nation's foundation were becoming more visible by the day. The Great Return, making it international law for all of England's immigrants to leave the island, was giving many in England exactly what they had wished for, for decades. They saw it as a chance of renewal, little had they anticipated the impact and scale of the remigrated diversity. A renewal, a cultural reformation was indeed on its way, but would be hugely influenced by the majority of returnees, not the minority native-born. It would not be easy for anyone. These returnees, with their diverse backgrounds and experiences, were struggling to find their place in a country that was increasingly divided along lines of class, origin, and identity. For example, returnees from the US east coast had very different ideals to people from the US west coast, yet they were forced to suddenly co-exist in the same slum.

For Sarah James, the work of documenting these developments was becoming both more urgent and more dangerous. The photo she had taken at the rally in London—of the mysterious operative linked to The Consortium—had been circulated widely, drawing attention not only to the growing unrest but also to the shadowy forces manipulating events from behind the scenes. But with that attention came increased scrutiny, and Sarah knew that she was now a target.

In the days following the rally, Sarah had been careful, avoiding her usual haunts and keeping a low profile. The warnings from The Fixer echoed in her mind, reminding her that she was walking a dangerous path. But the stories she was uncovering were too important to ignore, and she was determined to continue her work, no matter the risks.

One morning, as Sarah was preparing to head out for another day of interviews, she received a call from Victoria Langley, the MP she had been working with to expose the corruption linked to The Great Return. Langley had become a key ally in Sarah's investigation, using her political connections to quietly gather information and build a case against the officials and business interests involved.

"Sarah, we need to meet," Langley said, her voice tense. "I have something for you, but it needs to be handled carefully."

They agreed to meet in a small café in Westminster, a place

where they could talk without drawing too much attention. When Sarah arrived, she found Langley already seated in a quiet corner, a folder of documents in front of her. The MP looked more serious than usual, her expression reflecting the gravity of the situation.

As Sarah sat down, Langley pushed the folder across the table. "This is everything I've been able to gather so far. It's not complete, but it's enough to start putting the pieces together. The corruption runs deeper than we thought, and The Consortium is involved at every level."

Sarah opened the folder and began to sift through the documents. They included emails, financial records, and internal memos that linked key government officials to The Consortium and its network of shell companies. The evidence was damning, painting a picture of a government that was complicit in the exploitation of the returnees and the broader destabilisation of the country.

"This is incredible," Sarah said, her voice low. "But it's also dangerous. If this gets out, it could bring down the government."

"That's why we need to be careful," Langley replied. "We can't just publish this and hope for the best. We need to build a solid case, one that can't be dismissed or covered up. But we also need to act quickly—things are getting worse by the day, and I'm not sure how much longer we have before the situation spirals out of control."

Sarah nodded, understanding the urgency of the situation. The documents were a treasure trove of information, but they also represented a significant risk. The people involved were powerful, and they would not hesitate to protect themselves if they felt threatened.

"I'll start going through these right away," Sarah said, slipping the folder into her bag. "We need to find a way to get this out there without putting ourselves—and others—in danger."

Langley leaned in closer, her voice dropping to a whisper. "There are still people within the government who are on our side, but they're in the minority. The Consortium has its tentacles everywhere, and they've been tightening their grip ever since The Great Return began. We're dealing with something much bigger than just a few corrupt officials. This is about control—control of the country, control of the narrative, and control of the future."

Sarah felt a chill run down her spine. She had known from the beginning that The Consortium was a powerful force, but the extent of their influence was even more alarming than she had imagined. This was not just about money or power—it was about shaping the very identity of England, and the stakes could not be higher.

As they left the café, Sarah and Langley parted ways, each

aware of the dangers that lay ahead. Sarah made her way back to her anonymously owned flat, making sure she wasn't followed, her mind racing with the implications of what she had just learned. The country was teetering on the brink, and the decisions made in the coming days would determine its fate.

That evening, Sarah began to methodically go through the documents Langley had provided. As she pieced together the information, a clearer picture began to emerge. The Consortium's influence was far-reaching, extending into every corner of government and business. They had used The Great Return as a cover for their activities, exploiting the chaos to consolidate power and control.

One of the most troubling revelations was the extent to which The Consortium had manipulated the housing crisis. The contracts for the new developments, including those in places like New Haven, had been awarded to companies with direct ties to The Consortium. These companies had cut corners, using substandard materials and pocketing the difference, all while the returnees suffered in increasingly dire conditions.

The financial records also revealed a pattern of kickbacks and bribes, with key officials receiving substantial payments in exchange for their cooperation. The money had been funnelled through a complex web of offshore accounts, making it difficult to trace, but the evidence was there, hidden in plain sight.

Sarah's investigation also uncovered another disturbing fact: The Consortium had been actively fuelling the unrest that was spreading across the country. They had provided funding and support to nationalist groups like the National Unity Front, using them as a tool to sow division and destabilise the nation. The violence that had erupted in places like Birmingham and London was not spontaneous—it had been carefully orchestrated.

As Sarah worked late into the night, she felt a growing sense of urgency. The country was on the brink, and the forces driving the crisis were becoming more aggressive. The returnees, who had come to England with hopes of finding a new life, were being used as pawns in a much larger game. And the consequences of that game were becoming increasingly dire.

The next morning, Sarah received a message from The Fixer. It was brief, but the warning was clear: "They're closing in. Be ready."

The message sent a jolt of fear through Sarah, but it also steeled her resolve. She knew that she was getting close to something big, and that the risks were growing with each passing day. But she also knew that she couldn't stop now—not when the stakes were so high.

Later that day, Sarah met with Emily Carter again, the young returnee from Australia who had been caught up in the violence at the London rally. Emily had been shaken by the experience, but she was determined to continue her work supporting other returnees. The two women sat in a small café near the university where Emily had recently started a part-time job, talking about the challenges facing the returnees and the growing sense of alienation they felt.

"I never imagined it would be this hard," Emily said, her voice tinged with frustration. "I thought coming to England would be like coming home, but instead, it feels like we've walked into a war zone. People don't see us as part of the country—they see us as outsiders, as threats."

Sarah nodded, understanding all too well the difficulties Emily was facing. The promise of The Great Return had been one of unity and renewal, but the reality was far more complex. The returnees, with their diverse backgrounds and experiences, were challenging the very idea of what it meant to be English, and that challenge was being met with resistance.

"But we can't give up," Sarah said, her voice firm. "The only way things are going to change is if we keep pushing, keep telling our stories, and keep fighting for a future where everyone has a place. It's not going to be easy, but it's the only way forward."

Emily smiled, a flicker of hope in her eyes. "You're right. We can't let them win. This is our country too, and we're going to fight for it."

As they left the café, Sarah felt a renewed sense of purpose. The road ahead was going to be difficult, and the dangers were real, but she was not alone. There were others—like Emily, like Langley, like John McGuire—who were committed to fighting for a better future, a future where the fractures in the foundation could be repaired.

But as she walked through the streets of London, Sarah couldn't shake the feeling that the storm was still gathering, and that the worst was yet to come.

9

LINES DRAWN IN THE SAND

As the crisis in England deepened, the lines between friend and foe became increasingly blurred. The country was in the grip of a profound transformation, and the forces at play were pushing it toward an uncertain future. The Great Return, once seen by some as a chance to reconnect with heritage, was now a battleground where the very concept of Englishness was being contested. The returnees, with their diverse backgrounds and experiences, were both symbols of hope and catalysts for conflict.

Sarah James had uncovered enough to know that the situation was far more dangerous than most people realised. The Consortium's involvement in fuelling the unrest was no longer just a suspicion—it was a fact, supported by the documents Victoria Langley had provided. But knowing the truth and being able to act on it were two very different things. Sarah was keenly aware that the closer she got to exposing The Consortium, the greater the risk to her own safety.

One evening, as Sarah sat in her flat reviewing the latest round of interviews she had conducted, she received a message from Langley. It was urgent, asking her to meet in Windlesham, a location outside of London, away from prying eyes. The urgency of the message made Sarah's heart race. She knew that whatever Langley had discovered, it was critical.

The meeting place was a small, secluded pub around the corner from Westwood Road, far from the surveillance networks that had become ubiquitous in the city. When Sarah arrived, she found Langley sitting at a corner table, her expression grim. There was a tension in the air, an unspoken understanding that this meeting was about more than just the latest developments in their investigation.

As Sarah sat down, Langley leaned forward, her voice low. "We don't have much time. Things are moving quickly, and I've uncovered something that changes everything."

Sarah's heart pounded as Langley slid a small envelope across the table. Inside were photos and a brief report detailing the activities of several high-ranking government officials. The photos showed these officials meeting with known members of The Consortium, their expressions serious, their conversations clearly secretive.

But it was the report that chilled Sarah to the bone. It outlined a plan, already in motion, to escalate the unrest in key cities across England. The goal was to create a level of chaos that would justify the imposition of emergency powers—powers that would effectively suspend civil liberties and give the government, or more accurately, The Consortium, unprecedented control.

"They're planning a coup," Sarah whispered, her voice barely audible.

Langley nodded. "Not in the traditional sense, but yes. They want to destabilise the country to the point where they can step in as the 'saviours.' Once that happens, they'll have the power to reshape the nation in their image, with no opposition."

Sarah felt a wave of nausea. The implications were staggering. The violence, the unrest, the suffering—it was all part of a calculated strategy to seize control of the country. And they were running out of time to stop it.

"What do we do?" Sarah asked, her voice trembling slightly.

Langley looked at her, her eyes hard with determination. "We need to expose this before it's too late. We have to get this information to the right people—people who can act on it and prevent The Consortium from carrying out their plan. But we have to be careful. If they catch wind of what we're doing, they'll stop at nothing to silence us."

The weight of Langley's words pressed down on Sarah. She knew the risks, but the thought of doing nothing was unbearable. They had come too far to back down now.

As they left the pub, Langley handed Sarah a second envelope. "This is a list of people we can trust, people who are still loyal to the idea of a free and democratic England. Reach out to them, but be discreet. We can't afford any mistakes."

Sarah nodded, slipping the envelope into her bag. The list would be crucial in the coming days, as they tried to build a coalition strong enough to challenge The Consortium's plans.

Back in London, Sarah wasted no time. She began contacting the people on the list, setting up meetings and carefully vetting each contact. The work was gruelling, the constant fear of being discovered weighing heavily on her, but she pushed forward. The stakes were too high to allow fear to paralyse her.

One of the people on the list was David Ellison, a senior editor at a major newspaper who had earned a reputation for integrity and courage in his reporting. Sarah had met him a few times before, but their interactions had been brief and professional. Now, she needed to know if he could be trusted with the most explosive story of their careers.

They met in a quiet café, far from the prying eyes of The Consortium's agents. Sarah laid out what she had uncovered, showing David the documents, the photos, and the details of the plan to destabilise the country.

David listened intently, his face growing more serious with each passing minute. When Sarah finished, there was a long silence as he absorbed the information.

"This is big, Sarah," he finally said, his voice low. "If what you're saying is true, this could bring down the entire government. But it's also dangerous—more dangerous than anything I've ever worked on. We need to be absolutely certain before we publish anything. If we get this wrong, it could be disastrous."

Sarah nodded, understanding the gravity of the situation. They couldn't afford to make a mistake. The information had to be solid, the sources credible, and the timing perfect. Any misstep could give The Consortium the opportunity to discredit them, or worse.

"We need to verify everything," Sarah agreed. "But we also need to act quickly. They're planning something big, and we can't let them succeed."

David leaned back in his chair, his mind clearly racing. "I'll put my best people on it. We'll start verifying the documents, tracing the connections, and building the case. But we need to be careful—if The Consortium gets wind of this, they'll come after us hard."

Sarah knew he was right. The Consortium was ruthless, and they wouldn't hesitate to eliminate anyone who posed a threat to their plans. But the risk was worth it. If they could expose The Consortium before they could carry out their plan, they might just be able to save the country from descending into chaos.

As the days passed, Sarah and David's team worked tirelessly, piecing together the evidence and building a narrative that would expose The Consortium's machinations. The work was slow and painstaking, but the sense of urgency drove them forward. The unrest in the country was escalating, and time was running out.

Meanwhile, the situation on the ground was deteriorating rapidly. In cities across England, violence was flaring up with increasing frequency. The nationalist groups, emboldened by the support they were receiving from shadowy benefactors, were pushing their agenda with a new level of aggression. The returnees, caught in the middle, were facing growing hostility and suspicion.

Sarah continued her work on the ground, documenting the stories of those affected by the crisis. She met with Anna McDonald, a returnee from Australia who had recently moved to Birmingham with her family. Anna's story was one of many that reflected the growing sense of disillusionment among the returnees.

"Although forced to come here, we came with hope because we believed in the idea of England we had grown up with," Anna told Sarah during an interview in a small café near her home. "We thought we were coming back to a country that would welcome us, where we could reconnect with our roots. But instead, we've found ourselves in the middle of a nightmare. The violence, the hatred—it's tearing this country apart."

Sarah listened, her heart heavy with the weight of Anna's words. The hopeful returnees, who had come to England with dreams of building new lives, were now questioning their own aspirations. This had the effect of their dreams turning into nightmares. The country they had returned to was not the one they had imagined, and hope was rapidly sliding away.

As the interview concluded, Anna looked at Sarah, her eyes filled with a mixture of fear and determination. "We can't let them win," she said, her voice trembling. "This is our country too, and we have to fight for it."

Sarah nodded, feeling a renewed sense of purpose. Although there was no light at the end of the tunnel, people like Anna knew that survival meant moving forward, fervently seeking a route through the hopelessness.

That evening, as Sarah returned to her flat, she received another call from The Fixer.

"You're getting close," The Fixer said, her voice as calm as ever. "But be careful—The Consortium is aware of your latest investigative activities. They're starting to take precautions."

Sarah's heart skipped a beat. The warning was clear: she was now in real danger, and any misstep could be fatal.

"I understand," Sarah replied, her voice steady. "But we're not stopping. We're going to expose them."

"Good," The Fixer said. "But remember—trust no one, and keep moving. They'll try to isolate you, to cut you off from your allies. Don't let them."

The call ended, leaving Sarah with a sense of foreboding. The stakes were higher than ever, and the dangers more real. But the fight was too important to abandon. The future of England was hanging in the balance, and Sarah was determined to do everything in her power to tip the scales in favour of justice, laying the path forward to a healthy society.

Sarah worked late into the night, preparing for the final push. The storm was gathering, and the lines had been drawn. It was time take action.

10

THE TURNING POINT

The situation in England was reaching a critical juncture. The unrest that had begun as isolated incidents was now spreading like wildfire, fuelled by fear, misinformation, and the calculated manipulations of The Consortium. The country was teetering on the brink of chaos, and the choices made in the coming days would determine its fate. For Sarah James, the stakes had never been higher. She was now deeply embedded in the effort to expose The Consortium's plans, but with each step forward, the dangers grew more immediate and more personal.

In London, the city was on edge. The streets were filled with tension, with the uneasy quiet of a place bracing itself for something inevitable. The returnees, who had come to England seeking a new beginning, were finding themselves increasingly isolated, caught between the hostility of nationalist groups and the indifference of a government overwhelmed by the scale of the crisis. The English Dream, many returnees had, was gone, and the reality was a country violently divided. For decades, the Social Workers Party had been able to counter protests framed as the far-right. The SWP, as they were called, not a real political party, were well known to the police and had a slick machine that could be directed at any kind of nationalist right wing movement, disarming them through peaceful counter-protests as reminders that England was a country who welcomed diversity, immigrants and refugees.

Sarah herself had many friends in the SWP, but now they were nowhere to be seen, their mission totally lost in the chaos, as well as being short of funding which had gone to more pressing societal needs.

Sarah had been working tirelessly, her days blending into nights as she coordinated with David Ellison's team at the newspaper and continued her on-the-ground reporting. The information they had gathered was damning, but they knew that timing was everything. The Consortium's plan was already in motion, and they needed to act before it was too late.

One morning, Sarah received a call from David. His voice was urgent, the tension clear even over the phone.

"We've got a window, Sarah," he said. "But it's narrow. The government is planning to announce emergency measures tomorrow—measures that will effectively hand control over to The Consortium. If we're going to stop this, we need to publish today."

Sarah felt a jolt of adrenaline. The moment they had been preparing for was here. "I'll be there in an hour," she replied, already grabbing her bag and heading for the door.

When she arrived at the newspaper's office, the atmosphere was electric. The team was working at a frantic pace, finalising the story, verifying the last details, and preparing for what they knew would be a seismic revelation. David greeted her with a quick nod, his focus entirely on the task at hand.

"We've got everything lined up," he said, handing her a draft of the article. "Take a look and let me know if there's anything we've missed."

Sarah scanned the document, her mind racing as she absorbed the final details. The article laid out the full scope of The Consortium's plans, from their involvement in the housing crisis to their funding of nationalist groups and their ultimate goal of seizing control through emergency powers. The evidence was clear, the connections undeniable.

"This is it," Sarah said, her voice steady despite the gravity of the moment. "Let's do it."

David nodded, already signalling to his team to begin the publication process. "We're going live in thirty minutes. After that, we need to be ready for anything."

Sarah knew what he meant. The publication of this article would send shockwaves through the country, and the backlash would be swift. The Consortium would not take this lightly, and the risks to everyone involved were enormous. But there was no other choice. The truth had to be told, and it had to be told now.

As the countdown to publication began, Sarah reached out to Victoria Langley. The MP had been working behind the scenes to prepare for this moment, rallying allies within the government who were still committed to defending democracy and the rule of law.

"Are you ready?" Sarah asked when Langley answered the phone.

"We're ready," Langley replied, her voice firm. "As soon as the article goes live, we'll move. We've got a few key people in place who can help push back against the emergency measures. But it's going to be close."

Sarah knew what she meant. The forces aligned against them were powerful, and they had been preparing for this moment for a long time. The next few hours would be critical.

When the article finally went live, the response was immediate and overwhelming. The story quickly spread across social media, news outlets, and television, igniting a firestorm of reactions. The public, already on edge, was shocked by the revelations of corruption and manipulation at the highest levels of government. Protests erupted in cities across the country, with people taking to the streets to demand accountability and justice.

But even as the truth began to spread, the forces of The Consortium moved quickly to contain the damage. Within hours of the article's publication, the government announced the imposition of emergency powers, citing the need to restore order in the face of escalating violence. The measures were sweeping, effectively placing the country under martial law and giving The Consortium the control they had been seeking.

Sarah watched the news coverage in disbelief. Despite their efforts, it seemed that The Consortium had outmanoeuvred them, seizing the moment to consolidate their power. The country was in lockdown, and the backlash against the returnees was growing more intense by the hour.

But there was still hope. Langley and her allies within the government were working frantically to challenge the emergency measures, using the public outcry to push for a reversal. The situation was fluid, and the outcome was far from certain.

As the day wore on, Sarah received a message from The Fixer. It was brief, but the meaning was clear: "The fight isn't over. Meet me tonight."

The message filled Sarah with a renewed sense of purpose.

The fight was far from over, and she was determined to see it through. She knew that the risks were higher than ever, but the stakes were too important to ignore.

That evening, as the city remained in a tense lockdown, Sarah made her way secretively to the meeting place The Fixer had specified. It was a small, nondescript building in an industrial part of the city.

When she arrived, The Fixer was waiting for her, partially obscured by the shadows. There was an air of urgency in their demeanour, a sense that time was running out.

"The situation is worse than we thought," The Fixer said without preamble. "The Consortium is moving quickly to secure their control. They've already started rounding up key figures in the opposition, and they're using the unrest as an excuse to crack down on anyone who opposes them."

Sarah felt a chill run down her spine. The implications were clear: The Consortium was not just content with controlling the government—they were actively silencing dissent, eliminating any potential threats to their power.

"What do we do?" Sarah asked, her voice steady despite the fear gnawing at her.

"We have to go underground," The Fixer replied. "We've got allies, people who are still fighting, but we need to be smart about it. We can't confront them directly, not yet. We need to gather more evidence, build more support, and be on a war-footing. There's no guarantee or quick fix here."

Sarah nodded, understanding the gravity of the situation. The battle they were facing was not just about exposing the truth—it was about surviving long enough to see justice done.

Over the next few days, Sarah worked with The Fixer and their network of contacts to secure safe locations for key figures in the opposition, including Langley and other allies within the government. The Consortium's crackdown was swift and brutal, but there were still pockets of resistance, people who were willing to fight for the future of England.

The situation on the ground continued to deteriorate. The emergency measures had effectively silenced much of the media, and the streets were filled with armed patrols enforcing the lockdown. The returnees, who had already been facing hostility, were now being targeted by both nationalist groups and government forces, who saw them as convenient scapegoats for the unrest.

Sarah continued to document what she could, working in secret to gather evidence of the abuses being carried out under the guise of restoring order. The risks were enormous, but she knew that the information she was gathering could be crucial in the long-term fight against The Consortium.

As the days turned into weeks, the situation became increasingly dire. The country was under a de facto state of siege, with communication and travel severely restricted. But even in the face of such overwhelming odds, there were signs of hope. Small acts of resistance were occurring across the country—protests, strikes, and underground networks working to support those who had been targeted by The Consortium.

The future of England was hanging in the balance, and she was committed to doing everything in her power to ensure that justice and democracy would prevail.

As she prepared for another day of clandestine work, Sarah reflected on the journey she had taken since the beginning of The Great Return. The country she had grown up in, the country she had thought she understood, was being remade before her eyes. But even in the midst of chaos and uncertainty, she knew her very own humanity need to be part of the solution, paving the way to a truly healthy and reformed England.

For her, and the plan, the turning point had been reached, and there was no turning back.

11

RESILIENCE IN THE SHADOWS

The country was now firmly in the grip of The Consortium. The emergency measures had transformed England into a place Sarah barely recognised. Streets that were once bustling with life were now patrolled by armed forces, their presence a constant reminder of the new order that had taken hold. The media had been muzzled, dissent had been criminalised, and the returnees were living in fear as they became scapegoats for the unrest that continued to smoulder beneath the surface.

For Sarah James, the fight had moved underground. The truth that she and her allies had worked so hard to expose had been twisted by The Consortium into a justification for their draconian measures. But even in this darkest hour, there were still those who refused to give up hope, those who believed that England could be saved from the abyss it was rapidly descending into.

Sarah had gone into hiding, moving from one safe house to

another as she continued her work. The Fixer had proven invaluable, connecting her with a network of activists, journalists, and former government officials who were committed to resisting The Consortium's rule. These people, operating in the shadows, were the last line of defence for a free and just England.

One of the key figures in this underground movement was Eleanor Watts, a former intelligence officer who had resigned in protest when the emergency measures were imposed. Eleanor had been involved in counter-terrorism work for years, and she had seen firsthand how easily power could be abused. Now, she was using her skills to help coordinate the resistance, gathering intelligence on The Consortium's activities and finding ways to disrupt their operations.

When Sarah first met Eleanor, she was struck by the woman's calm demeanour and sharp mind. Eleanor was not one to be rattled easily, and she spoke with the confidence of someone who had faced down threats far more immediate than the one they were currently dealing with. But beneath her calm exterior, Sarah could sense a deep-seated anger—a determination to see justice done, no matter the cost.

"We're dealing with a sophisticated operation," Eleanor explained during one of their meetings. "The Consortium has resources and connections that go far beyond anything we've seen before. They've been planning this for years, and they're not going to give up control easily. But they've made one mistake—they've underestimated the resilience of the people they're trying to subdue."

Eleanor's words resonated with Sarah. Despite the overwhelming odds, there were still pockets of resistance across the country. Small acts of defiance—graffiti on walls, underground newspapers, secret gatherings—were occurring in towns and cities, keeping the spirit of resistance alive. These acts, though seemingly insignificant, were a reminder that The Consortium's grip on power was not absolute.

Sarah continued her work, documenting these acts of resistance and gathering evidence of The Consortium's abuses. She knew that one day, the truth would come out, and when it did, the world would need to know what had really happened. Her articles, smuggled out through a network of couriers and encrypted channels, were being published by sympathetic media outlets abroad, helping to keep the story alive in the underground social platforms.

One evening, while Sarah was working in yet another safe house, she received a message from The Fixer. It was brief, as always, but the message was clear: "We have a lead. Meet me tomorrow."

The next day, Sarah made her way to a small, nondescript building on the outskirts of the city. The area was largely abandoned, a relic of the industrial past, possibly about to spring to life again, as England was now a very poor nation and would need to manufacture for its own needs, only importing the very necessary items. The building provided the perfect cover for their clandestine meeting. When she arrived, The Fixer was already there, waiting as usual, in the shadows.

"I've found something," The Fixer said without preamble. "It's big. The Consortium's been moving assets out of the country—money, documents, people. They're preparing for something, and whatever it is, it's going to happen soon."

Sarah's mind raced. The Consortium's grip on power was tightening, but if they were moving assets out of the country, it could mean they were planning to escalate the situation even further—or worse, that they were preparing for an exit strategy, leaving England to collapse in their wake.

"Do we know where they're moving these assets?" Sarah asked, trying to keep her voice steady.

The Fixer nodded. "We've tracked some of it to offshore accounts, but the more worrying part is the people. They're moving key figures—scientists, engineers, military personnel—to undisclosed locations. They're building something, Sarah. Something big."

Sarah felt a cold knot form in her stomach. The implications were terrifying. Whatever The Consortium was planning, it was clear that they were not content with simply controlling England—they had a much larger agenda.

"We need to find out what they're building," Sarah said, her voice firm. "And we need to stop it."

The Fixer agreed. "We're working on it, but it's going to take time. In the meantime, we need to keep the resistance going. The more pressure we put on them, the more likely they are to make a mistake."

Over the next few weeks, Sarah threw herself into the work, coordinating with Eleanor and the rest of the underground network. The situation on the ground continued to deteriorate—more arrests, more crackdowns, more violence—but the resistance was growing. People who had once been too afraid to speak out were now finding the courage to join the fight.

One of the most significant developments came from within the military. A group of officers, disillusioned with the role they were being forced to play in enforcing The Consortium's will, had begun to quietly rebel. They were providing intelligence to the resistance, leaking documents that revealed the extent of The Consortium's control over the armed forces.

Sarah met with one of these officers, Captain James Morgan, in a remote location outside London. Captain Morgan had served in the military for over twenty years, and he had been a staunch defender of the government—until The Consortium had taken over.

"I joined the military to protect this country, not to turn it into a dictatorship," Morgan said, his voice filled with conviction. "What they're doing is wrong, and I won't be a part of it. But we can't fight them head-on. We need to be smart about this, find ways to weaken their control without putting more lives at risk."

Morgan provided Sarah with a trove of documents that detailed The Consortium's influence over the military, including plans for a massive expansion of the emergency powers that would effectively turn England into a police state. The documents also revealed a growing dissent within the ranks, with more and more soldiers questioning the orders they were being given.

As Sarah sifted through the documents, she realised that they held the key to turning the tide. The Consortium's power relied on the compliance of the military, and if that compliance could be undermined, their control would begin to crumble.

Eleanor and The Fixer agreed. The documents were a game-changer, and they began working on a plan to disseminate the information to the public. But they knew that the risks were enormous—if The Consortium discovered what they were doing, the consequences would be severe.

The plan they devised was risky but necessary. They would release the documents in stages, each leak designed to expose a different aspect of The Consortium's control. The goal was to create a groundswell of public outrage that would make it impossible for The Consortium to maintain their grip on power.

As the first wave of documents was released, the response was immediate. Despite the restrictions on the media, the information spread like wildfire through underground channels and social media. Protests erupted in cities across the country, and the pressure on The Consortium began to mount.

But The Consortium was not about to go down without a fight. They responded with a brutal crackdown, arresting hundreds of protesters and imposing even stricter controls on communication and travel. The country was in turmoil, and the line between order and chaos was becoming increasingly blurred.

Through it all, Sarah continued to document the resistance, knowing that every story she told, every act of defiance she recorded, was a blow against The Consortium's rule. The fight was far from over, and the road ahead was fraught with danger. But the resilience of the people she was working with, their determination to see justice done, gave her hope.

As the second wave of documents was prepared for release,

Sarah knew that they were approaching a critical moment. The Consortium was being backed into a corner, and they were becoming more desperate by the day. The fight for England's future was reaching its climax, and the outcome was anything but certain.

But one thing was clear: the good people of England were not going to go down without a fight. The spirit of resistance was alive and well, and it was growing stronger with each passing day.

The shadows were deepening, but within those shadows, there was still light—still hope.

12

THE FINAL PUSH

The situation in England had reached a tipping point. The Consortium's iron grip on the country was beginning to show cracks, but those in power were becoming more desperate and dangerous as they clung to control. The resistance, once fragmented and disorganised, was now coalescing into a force that could no longer be ignored. Sarah James, working tirelessly with her allies, knew that the time had come for the final push.

The underground network had grown stronger in recent weeks. The leaks of military documents, coordinated by Sarah, Eleanor, and Captain James Morgan, had ignited a firestorm of dissent across the country. Protests had spread from the cities to the countryside, and acts of defiance were becoming more frequent and more organised. The public was beginning to see The Consortium for what it truly was: a manipulative force that sought to subjugate the nation for its own gain.

But with each step forward, the risks grew. The Consortium had unleashed its full power in a desperate bid to maintain control. The crackdown was brutal, with mass arrests, violent repression of protests, and increased surveillance. The country was under de facto martial law, and the atmosphere was one of fear and uncertainty.

For Sarah, the work had become more dangerous than ever. She was constantly on the move, never staying in one place for too long. The safe houses that had once been sanctuaries were now potential traps, as The Consortium's agents hunted for those leading the resistance. But even in the face of this relentless pursuit, Sarah refused to back down. She knew that they were close to achieving something monumental, and she was determined to see it through to the end.

One evening, as Sarah was preparing to move to another location, she received a message from The Fixer. It was brief, but the urgency was unmistakable: "They're planning something big. Meet me tonight."

The meeting place was in the basement of an old warehouse on the outskirts of London. When Sarah arrived, she found The Fixer already there, along with Eleanor and Captain Morgan. The tension in the room was palpable; they all knew that whatever The Fixer had uncovered, it was critical.

"They're preparing for a final showdown," The Fixer began, their voice calm but laced with urgency. "The Consortium knows that they're losing control, and they're planning to escalate the situation in a way that could bring the country to its knees."

Sarah felt a chill run down her spine. "What are they planning?"

Eleanor spoke up, her expression grim. "They're going to stage a major incident—something that will justify even harsher measures. We're talking about a false flag operation, something that will make the public beg for the government to take total control."

Captain Morgan nodded in agreement. "We've seen indications that they're moving resources into place for a large-scale attack, something that will be blamed on the resistance or on the returnees. They want to create a scenario where they can completely dismantle what's left of civil liberties and crush any remaining opposition."

The gravity of the situation hit Sarah hard. The Consortium was willing to sacrifice innocent lives to maintain their power, and they were counting on the chaos to cement their rule. It was a terrifying prospect, one that could plunge the country into even deeper darkness.

"We have to stop this," Sarah said, her voice steady despite the fear gnawing at her. "But how? If they're planning something like this, they'll have every angle covered."

"We need to expose them before they can act," The Fixer

replied. "We've been gathering evidence, and we have enough to blow their plan wide open. But we need to be strategic about how we release it. If we move too soon, they'll shut us down before the truth can reach the public."

Eleanor leaned forward, her eyes locked on Sarah's. "This is the moment we've been building toward. We need to coordinate a massive release of information—documents, recordings, testimonies. We need to flood every channel we have, overwhelm their ability to suppress it. But we also need to ensure that the public understands what's happening, that they see through The Consortium's lies."

Captain Morgan added, "We've also been in contact with elements within the military who are ready to stand down, to refuse orders if it comes to that. But they need to see that the public is with them, that they're not alone in this."

The plan they devised was bold and fraught with danger. They would gather all the evidence they had, compiling it into a series of explosive reports that would be released simultaneously across multiple platforms—social media, underground news outlets, and international media. The goal was to reach as many people as possible, as quickly as possible, and to make it impossible for The Consortium to contain the fallout.

Sarah, Eleanor, and The Fixer worked through the night, coordinating with contacts across the country and beyond.

They knew that this was their last chance to stop The Consortium from carrying out their plan, and they threw everything they had into the effort.

As dawn broke, the final preparations were in place. The reports were ready, the channels secured, and the key players in the resistance had been briefed. Now, all they could do was wait for the right moment to strike.

That moment came sooner than they expected. Just hours after their final meeting, news broke of a supposed attack on a government facility in the north of England. The official narrative, hastily constructed, blamed the incident on "extremist elements" within the resistance movement. The media, under The Consortium's control, began broadcasting the story non-stop, fuelling public fear and anger.

But Sarah and her team were ready. Within minutes of the news breaking, they launched their counterattack. The evidence they had gathered—proof that the attack had been orchestrated by The Consortium itself—was released in a coordinated flood of information. Videos, documents, and eyewitness testimonies spread across the internet like wildfire, reaching millions of people within hours.

The reaction was immediate and explosive. Protests erupted across the country, with people demanding answers and accountability. The military, already uneasy with the orders they were being given, began to fracture, with some units refusing to carry out further operations against civilians.

The Consortium, caught off guard by the speed and scale of the resistance's response, scrambled to regain control. But it was too late. The truth was out, and the carefully constructed narrative they had relied on to maintain their power was unraveling.

In the midst of the chaos, Sarah continued to work, coordinating with her allies and documenting the events as they unfolded. She knew that they were far from out of danger—the situation was still volatile, and The Consortium was still capable of lashing out. But for the first time in weeks, she felt a glimmer of hope.

As the day wore on, the tide began to turn. The public, now aware of The Consortium's deception, began to rally behind the resistance. In cities and towns across the country, people took to the streets, demanding an end to the emergency measures and the restoration of democratic governance. The pressure on The Consortium was mounting, and cracks were beginning to appear in their once-solid facade.

In London, the heart of the resistance, a massive protest converged on Parliament. Sarah was there, her camera capturing the moment as thousands of people flooded the streets, their voices united in a call for justice. The energy was electric, the sense of purpose palpable. This was no longer just a fight against corruption—it was a fight for the soul of the nation.

As the protest reached its peak, Sarah received a message from The Fixer: "We've done it. They're falling back."

The news was almost too good to believe. The Consortium, faced with overwhelming public opposition and a fractured military, was retreating. The emergency measures were being lifted, and key figures within the government who had aligned themselves with The Consortium were being arrested. It was a stunning reversal, one that just days earlier had seemed impossible.

But even in this moment of triumph, Sarah knew that the fight was not over. The Consortium was a powerful and deeply entrenched force, and while they had been dealt a significant blow, they were not defeated. The road ahead would be long and difficult, with many challenges still to come.

That evening, as the protest began to disperse and the streets of London slowly returned to normal, Sarah found herself standing alone in the square where so much had happened. The weight of the past weeks pressed down on her, a mixture of exhaustion, relief, and a deep, abiding determination.

The final push had succeeded, but the work was far from finished. The country was at a crossroads, and the choices made in the coming days, weeks, and months would determine its future. But for the first time in a long time,

Sarah felt confident that the people of England were ready to fight for that future, to reclaim their country from those who had sought to exploit it.

As she walked through the quiet streets, Sarah reflected on the journey that had brought her to this point. The Great Return had been the catalyst for a series of events that had shaken the nation to its core, revealing the best and worst of what it meant to be English. But through it all, the spirit of resilience had endured, a reminder that no matter how dark the times, there was always hope.

The battle was not over, but the tide had turned. And as Sarah prepared for the challenges ahead, she knew that the fight for a better, more just England was one worth continuing.

13

AFTERMATH

The days following The Consortium's retreat were marked by a mixture of relief, uncertainty, and a simmering sense of tension. The emergency measures were gradually lifted, and the streets that had been under lockdown began to return to a semblance of normalcy. But the country was far from healed. The deep divisions and scars left by The Great Return and The Consortium's manipulations were still raw, and the future remained uncertain.

For Sarah James, the fight had moved into a new phase. The immediate threat posed by The Consortium had been neutralised, but the work of rebuilding the nation and holding those responsible to account was just beginning. The resistance had won a significant battle, but the war for England's soul was far from over.

In the days that followed, Sarah continued to document the stories of those affected by the crisis. The returnees, who had been caught in the crossfire of The Consortium's power grab, were now facing the challenge of integrating into a country that had been deeply shaken by the events of the past months. Many of them had come to England with dreams of a better life, only to find themselves in the midst of a nightmare. Now, as the country began to rebuild, they were struggling to find their place in a society that was still coming to terms with its own identity.

Sarah visited one of the temporary housing developments where many of the returnees had been living. The conditions, which had been dire even before The Consortium's crackdown, were now even worse. The infrastructure was crumbling, and resources were scarce. But despite the hardships, there was a sense of resilience among the people she met.

In one small, makeshift community hall, Sarah spoke with Emily Carter, the young returnee from Australia who had been active in supporting other returnees throughout the crisis. Emily had been one of the voices of hope during the darkest days, and now, as the country began to heal, she was determined to continue her work.

"We've been through hell," Emily said, her voice steady but filled with emotion. "But we're still here. And we're not giving up. This country is our home now, and we're going to fight to make it better—not just for ourselves, but for everyone who lives here."

Sarah was struck by Emily's determination. The returnees had faced incredible challenges, but they were not broken. Instead, they were emerging from the crisis with a renewed sense of purpose, determined to contribute to the rebuilding of the nation.

But not everyone was as hopeful. In other parts of the country, the divisions that had been exacerbated by The Great Return were still festering. The nationalist groups that had been empowered by The Consortium's manipulation were not simply fading away. Instead, they were regrouping, spreading their message of fear and division to those who were still struggling to come to terms with the changes that had swept through the country.

One evening, as Sarah was preparing to leave the housing development, she received a call from John McGuire, the union leader she had worked with throughout the crisis. John had been instrumental in rallying support for the resistance, and he was now turning his attention to the challenges of rebuilding the country's shattered social fabric.

"We've got a long road ahead of us," John said, his voice weary but resolute. "The Consortium might be on the back foot, but the damage they've done is going to take years to repair. We've got to stay vigilant, keep fighting for the rights of the people who've been hurt by all this. But we've also got to find a way to bring the country back together."

Sarah knew he was right. The battle against The Consortium had united many disparate groups under a common cause, but now that the immediate threat had receded, the old divisions were beginning to reassert themselves. The challenge of reconciliation—of finding a way to heal the deep wounds that had been inflicted on the nation—was going to be one of the hardest tasks they would face.

The next day, Sarah met with Victoria Langley at her office in Westminster. Langley, who had been one of the few voices in government to stand against The Consortium, was now playing a key role in the efforts to hold those responsible to account. But she was also deeply concerned about the future.

"The inquiry into The Consortium's activities is just beginning," Langley explained as they sat down in her cluttered office. "We've got a lot of evidence, thanks to you and your work, but the process of bringing these people to justice is going to be long and difficult. They're powerful, and they've still got allies in high places."

Sarah nodded, understanding the enormity of the task ahead. The Consortium might have been exposed, but they were not defeated. The fight to hold them accountable—to dismantle the networks of power and influence they had built—would be a marathon, not a sprint.

"We also have to think about the future," Langley continued. "The Great Return has brought up a lot of issues that this country has been avoiding for a long time—issues of identity, of what it means to be English in the 21st century. If we don't address those issues, if we don't find a way to bring people together, we're going to see this kind of division again."

Sarah agreed. The crisis had exposed the fault lines in English society, but it had also created an opportunity for change—for a reckoning with the past and a reimagining of the future. The question now was whether the country could seize that opportunity, or whether it would fall back into old patterns of division and exclusion.

In the weeks that followed, Sarah continued her work, documenting the ongoing efforts to rebuild and reconcile. She traveled to communities that had been torn apart by the crisis, listening to the stories of those who were trying to pick up the pieces of their lives. There were moments of hope—small victories in the fight to restore trust and solidarity—but there were also reminders of how fragile the situation remained.

One such moment came when Sarah visited a town in the north of England that had been one of the hardest hit by the unrest. The town had a large population of returnees, and tensions with the native-born residents had been high even before The Consortium's influence had exacerbated them. But now, in the aftermath of the crisis, something remarkable was happening.

In the centre of town, a group of local leaders—both returnees and native-born residents—had come together to create a new community initiative aimed at fostering dialogue and cooperation. They had started small, with meetings in the local community hall and joint projects to improve the town's infrastructure, but the impact was already being felt.

"We realised that we had more in common than we thought," said Margaret O'Neill, a long-time resident who had been involved in organising the initiative. "We were all struggling, all dealing with the same problems, but we were letting fear and suspicion drive us apart. Now, we're trying to change that, to build something better together."

The initiative was still in its early stages, and there were plenty of challenges ahead, but it was a sign that reconciliation was possible—that even in the most divided communities, there was a path forward.

As Sarah left the town, she felt a sense of cautious optimism. The road to recovery would be long and difficult, but there were signs that the country was beginning to heal. The returnees, who had been vilified and scapegoated, were finding allies among the native-born population, and together they were starting to rebuild the bonds that had been broken.

But even as the country began to move forward, Sarah knew

that the past could not be ignored. The inquiry into The Consortium's activities was just beginning, and the fight for justice would be long and arduous. The forces that had sought to divide and control the nation were still out there, and they would not go down without a fight.

As she prepared for the next phase of her work, Sarah reflected on the journey that had brought her to this point. The Great Return had been the catalyst for a series of events that had shaken the nation to its core, revealing the deep-seated issues that had been simmering beneath the surface for years. But it had also created an opportunity—a chance to confront those issues head-on and to build a better, more just society.

The country was still at a crossroads, and the choices made in the coming days, weeks, and months would determine its future. But Sarah was ready for the challenges ahead. She knew that the fight for justice, for reconciliation, and for the soul of the nation was one that would continue for a long time to come.

And as she looked out over the city from her flat that evening, she felt a renewed sense of purpose. The work was far from over, but the tide was turning. The people of England were beginning to reclaim their country, to heal the wounds that had been inflicted, and to build a future where everyone had a place.

The aftermath of the crisis would be difficult, but it was also a time of possibility—a time to reshape the nation and to ensure that the mistakes of the past were not repeated. And Sarah was determined to be a part of that process, to continue telling the stories that needed to be told, and to fight for the future of a country that was still finding its way.

14

REBUILDING TRUST

The process of rebuilding England was proving to be as challenging as the resistance had anticipated. While The Consortium had been pushed back and their immediate plans thwarted, the damage they had inflicted on the country was profound. The divisions they had exploited—between returnees and native-born citizens, between the powerful and the powerless—were not easily healed. Yet, there were signs of progress, fragile though they were.

For Sarah James, the work of documenting the nation's recovery had become a mission. The country was at a critical juncture, and the stories she told would play a role in shaping how England understood its past and envisioned its future. But the path forward was anything but clear, and every step was fraught with the potential for setbacks.

The inquiry into The Consortium's activities was slowly gaining momentum. Langley and her allies within the government were pushing hard to ensure that those responsible were held accountable, but the process was slow and complicated by the lingering influence of The Consortium's network. Many of the key players had gone underground or fled the country, and untangling the web of corruption and manipulation would take time.

In the meantime, the focus was shifting toward rebuilding trust—between communities, between the government and its citizens, and between the returnees and those who had long called England home. This was perhaps the greatest challenge of all, as the scars left by The Great Return were deep, and the wounds were still fresh.

Sarah's work took her to the Midlands, where she visited a town that had been deeply divided during the crisis. The town, Rotherham, had been a flashpoint for tensions between returnees and native-born residents, with clashes and protests occurring regularly. But in the aftermath of The Consortium's retreat, something unexpected was happening.

In Rotherham, a group of local leaders had come together to launch a new initiative aimed at rebuilding trust between the town's diverse communities. The initiative, called "One Rotherham", was focused on creating spaces for dialogue, understanding, and collaboration. It was a grassroots effort, born out of the realisation that the town's survival depended on its ability to overcome the divisions that had nearly torn it apart.

Sarah was introduced to Martha Graham, one of the founders of One Rotherham. Martha had lived in the town her entire life, and she had witnessed firsthand the impact of The Great Return and the ensuing unrest. But rather than give in to despair, Martha had decided to take action.

"We were on the brink of losing everything," Martha told Sarah as they sat in a small café that served as the group's unofficial meeting place. "People were angry, scared, and desperate. But we realised that if we didn't find a way to come together, we were going to destroy ourselves. One Rotherham is about more than just healing—it's about creating a future where we can all thrive, no matter where we come from."

The group's work was still in its early stages, but it was already making an impact. They had organised a series of community events—everything from town hall meetings to cultural festivals—designed to bring people together and foster a sense of shared purpose. The response had been overwhelmingly positive, with residents from all backgrounds coming forward to participate.

Sarah attended one of these events, a community dinner held in the town's central square. The atmosphere was lively, with long tables set up under strings of lights, and the air filled with the sounds of laughter and conversation. The food, contributed by local residents, represented the diverse culinary traditions of the town's inhabitants—traditional English dishes alongside Caribbean, Indian, and African cuisines, brought by those with primarily English DNA who had lived in various parts of the world.

As Sarah moved through the crowd, she spoke with several of the attendees, many of whom expressed a sense of cautious optimism. The memories of the crisis were still fresh, but there was a growing belief that the town could emerge stronger, more united than before.

James Cooper, a local business owner who had been skeptical of the returnees during the height of the crisis, was one of the people who had come around to the idea of One Rotherham.

"I'll admit, I wasn't sure about this at first," James said as they stood near one of the food tables. "But seeing everyone here, talking, sharing—it's starting to change my mind. Maybe we can find a way to make this work, after all."

Sarah was heartened by the stories she heard in Rotherham. The town was still facing significant challenges—economic hardship, lingering mistrust, and the slow process of rebuilding—but the spirit of cooperation she witnessed was a reminder that reconciliation was possible, even in the most divided communities.

But not all parts of the country were experiencing the same level of progress. In other towns and cities, the divisions remained stark, and the path to reconciliation was fraught with obstacles. The nationalist groups that had been emboldened during the crisis were still active, spreading their message of fear and exclusion to those who felt left behind by the changes sweeping the country.

In Bristol, Sarah encountered a community where the returnees were still viewed with suspicion and hostility. The local government, heavily influenced by nationalist rhetoric, had been slow to address the needs of the returnees, leaving them isolated and vulnerable. The result was a community on edge, with tensions simmering just below the surface.

Sarah met with Henry Parker, a returnee who had been living in Bristol for the past year. Henry's story was typical of many returnees who had been born abroad to English expatriates or had lived in former colonies, but who had primarily English DNA and had been compelled to return to England. Despite his best efforts to integrate and contribute to his new community, Henry had faced constant obstacles—discrimination in housing, difficulty finding work, and a pervasive sense of being unwelcome.

"I didn't have a choice," Henry said, his voice tinged with frustration and sadness. "The Global Repatriation Act made it clear that I had to return here because of my DNA. But it's been a struggle every step of the way. The people here—they look at me like I don't belong, like I'm an outsider in my own country."

Sarah could see the pain in Henry's eyes, a pain shared by many of the returnees she had spoken to in Bristol. The promise of The Great Return had turned into a nightmare for these individuals, as they grappled with the reality of a society that was not as open and welcoming as they had hoped.

The challenges faced by communities like Bristol were a stark reminder of the work that still needed to be done. The country was at a crossroads, with the potential to either heal and move forward or to fall back into the divisions that had nearly torn it apart.

As Sarah continued her reporting, she remained focused on the stories of those who were working to bridge the divides. The path to reconciliation was long and uncertain, but there were signs of hope—communities coming together, individuals stepping up to lead, and a growing recognition that the future of England depended on its ability to embrace its diversity.

One such sign came from an unexpected source—the military. Captain James Morgan, who had played a key role in the resistance against The Consortium, was now leading an effort within the armed forces to address the divisions that had been exposed during the crisis. He had organised a series of workshops and training programs aimed at fostering understanding and cooperation among soldiers from different backgrounds, with a focus on building a military that reflected the values of a democratic and inclusive society.

"We can't afford to go back to the way things were," Captain Morgan told Sarah during an interview at a military base in the south of England. "The crisis showed us just how fragile our society is, and how easily it can be torn apart by fear and prejudice. It's our responsibility to make sure that never happens again."

The work being done by Captain Morgan and others like him was a testament to the resilience of the nation. The road ahead was still fraught with challenges, but there were people across the country who were committed to building a better future—one that was not defined by the divisions of the past, but by the shared values of justice, equality, and unity.

As Sarah prepared to write her next series of articles, she reflected on the journey that had brought her to this point. The Great Return had been the catalyst for a seismic shift in the nation's identity, revealing both the best and worst of what it meant to be English. But through it all, the spirit of resilience had endured, a reminder that even in the darkest times, there was always hope.

The country was still finding its way, still grappling with the legacy of the crisis, but there was a growing belief that a better future was possible. And as Sarah continued her work, she was determined to be a part of that future—to tell the stories that needed to be told, to hold those in power accountable, and to fight for a nation that was just, inclusive, and united.

The process of rebuilding trust would be long and difficult, but it was a task worth undertaking. England was at a crossroads, and the choices made in the coming days, weeks, and months would determine its future. But with each step forward, Sarah felt a renewed sense of purpose, a belief that the country could emerge from the crisis stronger and more united than before.

15

NEW BEGINNINGS

The road to recovery was long and winding, and the process of rebuilding England in the aftermath of The Great Return was far from complete. The country was slowly finding its footing, but the scars of the past were still visible, and the challenges ahead were immense. However, amid the uncertainty, there were also signs of renewal—of communities coming together, of new initiatives being launched, and of people finding ways to move forward.

For Sarah James, the stories she was uncovering were a testament to the resilience and determination of the people she encountered. The crisis had exposed the deep divisions within English society, but it had also revealed the strength of those who were committed to overcoming those divisions and building a better future.

In London, where the initial impact of The Great Return had been felt most acutely, a new initiative was taking shape. The city, still grappling with the influx of returnees and the legacy of The Consortium's manipulations, was at the forefront of efforts to create a more inclusive and equitable society. At the heart of this movement was a group known as The New London Collective.

The New London Collective was a diverse group of returnees and native-born Londoners who had come together with a common goal: to transform the city into a place where everyone could thrive, regardless of their background. The group was focused on addressing the economic and social challenges facing the city, with a particular emphasis on housing, employment, and community cohesion.

Sarah was introduced to Dr. Olivia Bennett, one of the founding members of The New London Collective. Dr. Bennett was a sociologist who had returned to England from Canada, where her family had lived for generations. With over 70% English DNA, Dr. Bennett had been among the first wave of returnees, and she had quickly become involved in efforts to support others who were struggling to adapt to life in the country.

"We saw an opportunity to do something different," Dr. Bennett explained as they walked through a neighbourhood in East London where The New London Collective had been working. "The crisis revealed how fragile our society was, how easily it could be torn apart by fear and division. But it also showed us that there's a hunger for change, for a new way of doing things. That's what we're trying to build—a new London, where everyone has a stake in the future."

The Collective's work was multifaceted. They were involved in everything from organising community events and job fairs to advocating for policy changes at the local and national levels. One of their most ambitious projects was a plan to convert abandoned buildings and unused land into affordable housing for returnees and low-income residents.

Sarah visited one of these projects, a former industrial site that was being transformed into a vibrant community hub. The site, which had been derelict for years, was now buzzing with activity as volunteers worked to renovate the buildings and create spaces for housing, workshops, and social enterprises.

Thomas Evans, a young architect who had returned to England from South Africa, was leading the design and construction efforts. Thomas, whose English DNA was just over 65%, had initially struggled to find work in his field after returning to London. But through The New London Collective, he had found a way to use his skills to make a difference.

"This project is about more than just housing," Thomas told Sarah as they walked through the site. "It's about creating a sense of community, about bringing people together and showing them that we can build something better if we work together. We're not just fixing up old buildings—we're laying the foundation for a new way of living."

The project was still in its early stages, but the impact was already being felt. The first residents had moved in, and the sense of hope and possibility was palpable. For many of the returnees, who had experienced rejection and isolation upon their arrival, this new community offered a chance to start over, to build a life in a city that was beginning to embrace them.

Sarah was deeply moved by what she saw. The work being done by The New London Collective was a powerful reminder that even in the midst of crisis, there was potential for renewal. The city, like the country as a whole, was still grappling with the challenges of integration and reconciliation, but there were people who were committed to making it work.

But even as she documented these stories of hope, Sarah was acutely aware of the challenges that remained. The divisions that had been exposed by The Great Return were not going to disappear overnight. In many parts of the country, the returnees were still viewed with suspicion, and the nationalist rhetoric that had gained traction during the crisis was still a powerful force.

In Manchester, Sarah encountered a different kind of struggle. The city, with its rich industrial history and diverse population, had been a microcosm of the broader national crisis. The returnees in Manchester had faced significant challenges, not just in terms of finding housing and employment, but in navigating a social landscape that was often hostile to outsiders, even those with English DNA.

Sarah met with William Turner, a historian who had returned to Manchester after spending most of his life in Australia. William's family had left England generations ago, but his DNA test had shown a strong English lineage, compelling him to return under the Global Repatriation Act. Despite his deep connection to England's history, William had struggled to find his place in the city.

"It's been difficult," William admitted as they walked through a museum where he had recently started working as a curator. "I've always felt English, even when I was living abroad. But coming back here, I've realised that the England I imagined doesn't really exist anymore. The country has changed, and in some ways, it feels like I'm a stranger in my own homeland."

But William was not giving up. He had joined a group of historians and cultural workers who were dedicated to preserving and reinterpreting England's history in a way that reflected the realities of the 21st century. Their work was focused on creating a more inclusive narrative, one that acknowledged the contributions of returnees and immigrants while also confronting the darker aspects of the nation's past. "We can't move forward unless we understand where we've come from," William said, his voice resolute. "The Great Return has forced us to reckon with our history in a way that we've never had to before. It's painful, but it's necessary. If we're going to build a future where everyone feels they belong, we have to start by telling the truth about our past."

The work being done in Manchester was a testament to the complexity of the challenges facing the country. Reconciliation was not just about building new communities or creating economic opportunities—it was about addressing the deep-rooted issues of identity and belonging that had been brought to the surface by The Great Return.

As Sarah continued her journey across the country, she found herself reflecting on the enormity of the task ahead. The stories she was telling were important, but they were just one piece of a much larger puzzle. The future of England would be shaped not just by the actions of those in power, but by the everyday decisions and interactions of people in communities large and small.

The New London Collective, the historians in Manchester, the grassroots efforts in towns like Rotherham—these were the building blocks of a new England, one that was still taking shape. The road ahead would be long and difficult, but there was a growing sense that the country was finally beginning to confront the challenges it had long ignored.

As Sarah prepared to return to London, she felt a renewed sense of purpose. The work of rebuilding and reconciliation was just beginning, but she was determined to be a part of it. The stories she was telling were not just about the past—they were about the future, about the possibilities that lay ahead for a country that was still finding its way.

England was at a crossroads, and the choices made in the coming days, weeks, and months would determine its future. But with each step forward, Sarah felt a growing belief that the country could emerge from the crisis stronger, more united, and more just.

16

THE GATHERING STRENGTH

As England continued to rebuild, there was a growing realisation that the challenges ahead would require not just resilience but also innovation, cooperation, and a new way of thinking about identity and community. The scars left by The Great Return and The Consortium's manipulations were still raw, but there was a sense that the country was beginning to gather strength, to find a way forward that could address the deep-seated issues that had been brought to the surface.

For Sarah James, the stories she was uncovering reflected a nation at a crossroads. The efforts to rebuild communities, to foster reconciliation, and to create a more just and inclusive society were gaining momentum, but they were also facing significant resistance. The old divisions had not disappeared, and the forces that had sought to exploit them were still active, albeit more covertly.

In the weeks following her return from Manchester, Sarah found herself increasingly focused on the ways in which different regions of England were responding to the new realities of The Great Return. The country's diversity, once a source of strength, had become a point of contention during the crisis, and now it was at the centre of efforts to redefine what it meant to be English in the 21st century.

One of the most intriguing developments was taking place in Cornwall, a region with a distinct cultural identity and a long history of independence. The returnees in Cornwall, many of whom had Cornish ancestry, had been among the most resistant to the idea of being "forced" to return under the Global Repatriation Act. However, the region had also been one of the most successful in integrating returnees and creating a sense of shared purpose.

Sarah traveled to Cornwall to meet with Gareth Perran, a local leader who had been instrumental in bringing together returnees and native-born residents. Gareth, whose family had lived in Cornwall for generations, had been skeptical of The Great Return at first, seeing it as an imposition on the region's unique identity. But over time, he had come to see the returnees as a valuable part of the community, bringing new energy and ideas to a region that had long struggled with economic challenges.

"We've always been a bit different down here," Gareth said with a wry smile as they walked along the rugged coastline. "Cornwall has its own language, its own traditions, and for a long time, we've felt like we were a bit separate from the rest of England. But the returnees—they've brought something new to the table. They've reminded us that being Cornish and being English aren't mutually exclusive."

Gareth had worked with local councils and community organisations to create programs that helped returnees integrate into Cornish society, while also preserving and promoting the region's unique cultural heritage. The result was a flourishing of new initiatives, from small businesses to cultural festivals, that were helping to revitalise the region.

Sarah visited one of these initiatives, a cooperative farm that had been started by a group of returnees and local farmers. The farm, which focused on sustainable agriculture and traditional Cornish farming methods, had quickly become a model for other communities looking to blend old and new practices.

Sophie Trevithick, one of the returnees involved in the project, had returned to Cornwall from Australia, where her family had lived for decades. With over 80% Cornish DNA, Sophie had been drawn to the region by the promise of reconnecting with her roots, but she had also brought with her a wealth of experience in sustainable farming techniques.

"We're trying to create something that honours the past but also looks to the future," Sophie explained as they toured the farm. "The land here is special, and we want to make sure it's preserved for future generations. But we're also trying to show that there's a way to do things that's both traditional and innovative."

The farm was a success story, one that had drawn attention from other regions looking for ways to integrate returnees and revitalise local economies. But it was also a reminder that the process of reconciliation and renewal was not just about policy—it was about people finding common ground and working together to build something better.

As Sarah continued her reporting in Cornwall, she was struck by the sense of possibility that permeated the region. The challenges were still there—economic hardship, cultural tensions, and the lingering effects of The Great Return—but there was also a sense that Cornwall was beginning to find its way, to carve out a new identity that was both rooted in tradition and open to the future.

But not all parts of the country were experiencing the same sense of renewal. In the Midlands, Sarah encountered a different reality. The region, which had been hit hard by the economic downturn and the social upheaval of The Great Return, was struggling to regain its footing. The returnees in the Midlands, many of whom had come from former British colonies in Africa and Asia, were facing significant challenges in terms of housing, employment, and social integration.

Sarah met with Amelia Singh, a returnee who had come to

the Midlands from Kenya, where her family had lived for several generations. With her DNA showing a strong English heritage, Amelia had been required to return under the Global Repatriation Act. However, her experience in the Midlands had been marked by a sense of alienation and frustration.

"It's been hard," Amelia admitted as they sat in a small café in Birmingham. "I was excited to come back, to reconnect with my English roots, but it hasn't been what I expected. People look at me and don't see someone who belongs here, even though my DNA says otherwise. It's like I'm caught between two worlds—neither fully Kenyan nor fully English."

Amelia's story was emblematic of the challenges faced by many returnees in the Midlands. Despite their strong ties to England through their DNA, they were often seen as outsiders, as people who didn't quite fit into the social fabric of the region. The economic challenges only compounded the issue, with many returnees struggling to find stable employment and affordable housing.

But even in the face of these challenges, there were signs of hope. Amelia had recently become involved in a community initiative aimed at fostering understanding and cooperation between returnees and native-born residents. The initiative, known as "New Beginnings," was focused on creating spaces for dialogue and collaboration, with the goal of breaking down the barriers that had been erected during the crisis.

"We're trying to build bridges," Amelia said, her voice filled with determination. "It's not easy, and there's a lot of work to be done, but I believe we can create something better. We just need to keep talking, keep working together, and keep believing that things can change."

Sarah was inspired by Amelia's resilience and the efforts of others in the Midlands who were working to create a more inclusive and supportive community. The road ahead was long, but there were people who were committed to making it work, to ensuring that the promises of The Great Return were not just empty words.

As Sarah returned to London, she felt a renewed sense of purpose. The stories she had uncovered in Cornwall and the Midlands were a reminder that the process of rebuilding and reconciliation was complex and multifaceted. It was not just about economic recovery or social integration—it was about redefining what it meant to be English in a country that was still grappling with its identity.

The work of reconciliation was far from over, but the strength of the people she had met—their determination, their resilience, and their willingness to find common ground—gave her hope. England was still finding its way, but it was beginning to gather strength, to build a future that was rooted in both tradition and innovation.

As Sarah prepared to write her next series of articles, she reflected on the journey that had brought her to this point. The Great Return had been the catalyst for a seismic shift in the nation's identity, revealing both the best and worst of what it meant to be English. But through it all, the spirit of resilience had endured, a reminder that even in the darkest times, there was always hope.

The country was still at a crossroads, and the choices made in the coming days, weeks, and months would determine its future. But with each step forward, Sarah felt a growing belief that the country could emerge from the crisis stronger, more united. The English dream could be one that once again, offered hope.

17

THE ROAD AHEAD

The process of rebuilding England was gaining momentum, but the path forward was still uncertain and fraught with challenges. The country was beginning to heal from the immediate effects of The Great Return and The Consortium's manipulations, but the deeper issues of identity, belonging, and historical injustice remained unresolved. As the nation grappled with these complex questions, there was a growing recognition that the road ahead would be long and difficult, but also filled with possibilities for renewal and transformation.

For Sarah James, the stories she had uncovered so far had painted a picture of a country in the midst of profound change. From the grassroots initiatives in communities across England to the efforts to confront the nation's imperial past, there was a sense that the country was beginning to reckon with its history and to chart a new course for the future. But the work of reconciliation and renewal was far from over, and the challenges that lay ahead were formidable.

One of the most pressing challenges was the question of how to integrate the millions of returnees who had come to England under the Global Repatriation Act. These individuals, compelled to return by their English DNA, had brought with them diverse experiences, cultures, and perspectives. But their presence had also sparked tensions and raised difficult questions about what it meant to be English in the 21st century.

In Birmingham, one of the cities that had experienced significant social upheaval during The Great Return, efforts were underway to address these questions head-on. The city, known for its diverse population and history of immigration, was at the forefront of efforts to create a more inclusive and cohesive society.

Sarah traveled to Birmingham to meet with Georgina Stuart, a community organiser who had returned to England from Australia. Georgina's family had lived in Adelaide for generations, her, and her family's remigration had really hurt as they left their wine farm in the Adelaide Hills, although they were paid out, it was in ecoins and amounted to very little due to the strength of the Aussie dollar. Despite the challenges she had faced upon her arrival, Georgina had quickly become a leading figure in efforts to integrate returnees and foster dialogue between different communities.

"We're trying to build something new here," Georgina explained as they walked through a bustling market in the heart of Birmingham. "The crisis showed us how fragile our society is, but it also showed us the potential to thrive. We're working to create a city where everyone feels they belong, where people can bring their whole selves to the table and contribute to building a better future."

Georgina was involved in a number of initiatives aimed at promoting social cohesion and economic inclusion. One of the most successful was a program that paired returnees with local mentors who could help them navigate the complexities of life in England. The program, known as "Bridges," had already helped hundreds of returnees find housing, employment, and a sense of community.

Sarah visited one of the programme's workshops, where returnees were learning skills that would help them integrate into the local economy. The atmosphere was lively, with participants exchanging stories and tips as they worked on projects ranging from job applications to small business plans. The sense of camaraderie and mutual support was palpable, a testament to the power of community in the face of adversity.

Miriam Fletcher, a returnee from South Africa, was one of

the participants in the program. Miriam's family had left England generations ago, but her DNA had brought her back to a country that she had only known through stories. The adjustment had been difficult, but the Bridges program had provided her with the support she needed to start building a new life.

"This has been a lifeline for me," Miriam said as they sat down for a break. "Coming back to England was overwhelming at first—I didn't know where to start. But being part of this program, meeting other returnees, and connecting with people who understand what I'm going through—it's made all the difference. I feel like I'm starting to find my place here."

Miriam's story was one of many that highlighted the importance of initiatives like Bridges in helping returnees integrate into English society. But it also underscored the challenges that remained. The process of rebuilding trust and creating a sense of belonging for all was still in its early stages, and there were significant obstacles to overcome.

One of the biggest challenges was the persistence of nationalist rhetoric and exclusionary attitudes in some parts of the country. While cities like Birmingham were making strides in fostering inclusion, other regions were struggling with the legacy of division and fear that had been exacerbated by The Great Return.

In Kent, Sarah encountered a community that was grappling with these issues in a particularly acute way. The county, with its proximity to mainland Europe, had long been a gateway for migrants and returnees. But it had also been a hotbed of nationalist sentiment, with many residents feeling threatened by the changes that The Great Return had brought.

Sarah met with Robert Dean, a local councillor who had been working to address the tensions in the community. Robert, a lifelong resident of Kent, had initially been skeptical of the returnees, seeing them as a potential threat to the region's way of life. But over time, he had come to realise that the challenges facing Kent were not about the returnees themselves, but about the fear and uncertainty that had been stoked by The Consortium and other forces.

"We've got a lot of work to do here," Robert admitted as they walked through a quiet village on the outskirts of Canterbury. "There's a lot of fear, a lot of anxiety about the future. People are worried about their jobs, about their homes, about the changes they see happening around them. But I've also seen that when people come together, when they start talking to each other and finding common ground, things can change."

Robert had helped launch a series of community dialogues aimed at bringing together returnees and long-time residents to discuss their concerns and find ways to work together. The dialogues, which had been met with some resistance at first, were beginning to make a difference. Slowly but surely, the walls of suspicion and fear were starting to come down, replaced by a growing sense of mutual understanding and respect.

Sarah attended one of these dialogues, held in a local community hall. The atmosphere was tense at first, with participants expressing a range of emotions, from frustration to fear to hope. But as the conversation unfolded, there was a noticeable shift. People began to listen to each other, to share their stories and their hopes for the future. By the end of the evening, there was a sense that something important had begun—that the community was starting to heal.

As Sarah left Kent, she reflected on the challenges and opportunities that lay ahead for England. The road to reconciliation and renewal was long and difficult, but there were signs that the country was beginning to find its way. The efforts to integrate returnees, to foster dialogue, and to confront the past were all part of a larger process of transformation—one that would ultimately determine the future of the nation.

18

THE RECKONING

As England continued to navigate its post-crisis recovery, the time for a reckoning had arrived. The country had made significant strides in rebuilding its social fabric and addressing the deep divisions exposed by The Great Return, but the forces that had sought to exploit those divisions were still at large. The Consortium, although weakened, had not been fully dismantled, and the individuals and institutions that had supported its rise to power remained a threat to the nation's fragile recovery.

For Sarah James, the focus of her work had shifted. She had spent months documenting the resilience of communities, the efforts to integrate returnees, and the ongoing struggle to redefine English identity. Now, she was determined to turn her attention to the pursuit of justice. The stories she had uncovered had highlighted the courage and determination of ordinary people, but they had also revealed the extent of the damage caused by The Consortium and its allies. It was time to hold those responsible to account.

The inquiry into The Consortium's activities, led by Victoria Langley and her allies within the government, had been making slow but steady progress. The evidence gathered by Sarah and others had played a crucial role in exposing the network of corruption, manipulation, and abuse that had allowed The Consortium to gain so much power. But the process of bringing those responsible to justice was fraught with challenges. Many of the key figures had gone underground, and others were using their remaining influence to obstruct the inquiry and evade accountability.

In London, the heart of the inquiry's operations, Sarah met with Langley to discuss the latest developments. The atmosphere in Langley's office was tense, a reflection of the immense pressure they were under to deliver results. The public's demand for justice was growing louder by the day, but the obstacles they faced were formidable.

"We're up against some of the most powerful people in the country," Langley said, her voice a mix of determination and frustration. "They've got resources, connections, and they're not going down without a fight. But we've got the truth on our side, and we've got the people behind us. We just need to keep pushing."

Langley outlined the next steps in the inquiry, which included a series of high-profile hearings that would bring key witnesses to testify about The Consortium's activities. These hearings were expected to be explosive, with the potential to reveal the full extent of the corruption and abuses that had taken place. But they were also risky. The Consortium still had allies in powerful positions, and there were concerns about the safety of those who were willing to speak out.

Sarah agreed to continue her work documenting the inquiry and providing support to those who were coming forward. She knew that the road to justice would be long and difficult, but she was committed to seeing it through. The truth had to be told, and those responsible had to be held accountable.

The first of the hearings took place in a packed courtroom in central London. The atmosphere was electric, with journalists, activists, and members of the public all eager to hear the testimony that would be presented. The proceedings were broadcast live, and millions of people across the country tuned in to watch as the story of The Consortium's rise and fall was laid bare.

One of the key witnesses was Thomas Slate, a former executive within The Consortium who had decided to cooperate with the inquiry in exchange for immunity from prosecution. Slate's testimony was damning, detailing the inner workings of The Consortium, the methods they had used to manipulate public opinion, and the collusion between corporate interests and government officials that had allowed them to operate with impunity.

As Slate spoke, the full extent of The Consortium's reach became clear. Their influence had extended into nearly every aspect of British society—politics, media, finance, and even the judiciary. They had exploited the fear and uncertainty generated by The Great Return to further their own agenda, using nationalist rhetoric and scapegoating the returnees to distract from their true intentions.

The revelations sparked outrage across the country. Protests erupted in cities and towns, with people demanding that those responsible be brought to justice. The hearings continued for several weeks, with more witnesses coming forward to provide evidence of The Consortium's activities. The inquiry was uncovering a web of corruption that went far beyond what anyone had initially suspected.

But the fight for justice was not without its dangers. As the inquiry gained momentum, there were increasing reports of threats and intimidation against witnesses, journalists, and members of the inquiry team. Sarah herself was not immune. One evening, as she was leaving the inquiry offices, she noticed a car following her. The driver made no attempt to conceal their presence, a clear warning that she was being watched.

Undeterred, Sarah pressed on. She knew that the risks were

high, but she also knew that the work they were doing was too important to abandon. The country's future depended on their ability to hold those responsible to account and to ensure that the abuses of the past would not be repeated.

As the inquiry moved into its final phase, the focus shifted to the question of accountability. The evidence was overwhelming, and public pressure was mounting for the government to take action. But the question of how to bring those responsible to justice was complex. Many of the key figures had fled the country, and others were hiding behind layers of legal protection and political influence.

Langley and her team were working tirelessly to navigate these challenges. They were pursuing international warrants, freezing assets, and negotiating with foreign governments to secure the extradition of those who had fled. But the process was slow, and there were concerns that some of the most powerful figures might escape justice altogether.

One of the most notorious figures in The Consortium was Richard Blake, a billionaire financier who had been one of the chief architects of the organisation's rise to power. Blake had fled to an island in, what was now, a very empty Caribbean, as soon as the inquiry began. He had used his considerable resources to avoid capture and remigration. Despite this, Langley was determined to bring him to justice.

"We can't let him get away," Langley said during a meeting

with Sarah and other members of the inquiry team. "Blake is the key to unraveling the entire network. If we can get him, we can bring down the rest."

The efforts to track down Blake became a focal point of the inquiry's final phase. Langley's team worked with international GMU enforcement agencies, private investigators, and even former intelligence operatives to locate Blake and build a case against him. The pursuit was relentless, and the tension was palpable as they closed in on their target.

Finally, after weeks of intensive work, Langley received the news she had been waiting for. Blake had been located, and a plan was in place to arrest him. The operation, coordinated with GMU approval, was carried out swiftly and without incident. Blake was taken into custody and remigrated to the UK to face charges.

The arrest of Richard Blake marked a turning point in the inquiry. With Blake in custody, the inquiry team was able to gather crucial evidence that led to the arrest of several other high-ranking members of The Consortium. The network of corruption and abuse that had plagued the country for so long was finally being dismantled.

As the inquiry reached its conclusion, there was a sense of both relief and determination. The fight for justice was not over, but the most dangerous elements of The Consortium had been neutralised. The country was beginning to heal, and there was hope that the lessons of the past would lead to a more just and equitable future.

Sarah had witnessed the courage and resilience of ordinary people, the power of truth, and the importance of holding those in power accountable. The story of The Great Return and its aftermath was one of pain and struggle, but it was also a story of hope and renewal.

As Sarah prepared to write the final chapter of her coverage, she reflected on the lessons she had learned. The work of rebuilding and reconciliation was far from over, but the country was on a path toward healing. The reckoning with the past had been painful, but it was also necessary. It was a reminder that justice, though sometimes slow and difficult, was worth fighting for.

The road ahead was still uncertain, but Sarah felt a renewed sense of purpose. The country was beginning to find its way, to build a future that was rooted in truth, justice, and accountability. Sarah was finally able to dream the English dream she had always wanted for herself, loved ones and society.

EPILOGUE: THE LEGACY OF THE GREAT RETURN

A year had passed since the final chapter of The Great Return, and England was a country transformed. The nation was still healing, still grappling with the challenges of integration, reconciliation, and justice, but there was a growing sense of hope and possibility. The work that had begun in the aftermath of the crisis was now bearing fruit, as communities across the country came together to build a future rooted in the lessons of the past.

For Sarah James, the past year had been a time of reflection and growth. Her work as a journalist had brought her to the heart of one of the most significant events in modern British history, and the stories she had uncovered had shaped the national conversation. But as the country moved forward, Sarah found herself looking to the future with a sense of renewed purpose.

The inquiry into The Consortium's activities had led to a series of high-profile trials, with several key figures receiving lengthy prison sentences for their roles in the corruption and abuses that had nearly torn the country apart. The trials had been a powerful reminder of the importance of accountability and the rule of law, and they had provided a sense of closure for many who had suffered during the crisis.

But the legacy of The Great Return was not just about justice for the past—it was also about building a better future. Across England, new initiatives were taking root, inspired by the resilience and determination of the people who had come together during the crisis. Community organisations, educational programs, and social enterprises were flourishing, helping to bridge the divides that had once seemed insurmountable.

In London, The New London Collective had expanded its reach, launching new projects focused on housing, education, and cultural exchange. The city, which had been at the epicentre of the crisis, was now leading the way in creating a more inclusive and vibrant society. The collective's work had become a model for other cities and regions, and there was a growing sense that London was once again the beating heart of a nation in transformation.

In Manchester, Birmingham, and other cities, similar efforts were underway. The returnees, who had once been seen as outsiders, were now integral parts of their communities, contributing to the social and economic renewal that was sweeping the country. The Bridges program in Birmingham had expanded to rural areas, helping to create connections between returnees and long-time residents in even the most isolated parts of the country.

The process of reconciliation and renewal was not without its challenges. There were still pockets of resistance, still those who clung to the old ways of thinking, still those who feared the changes that were taking place. But the momentum was on the side of progress, and there was a growing belief that the future could be brighter, more just, and more inclusive.

For Sarah, the stories she had told over the past year had left a deep impression on her. She had seen the best and worst of humanity, the depths of division and the heights of resilience. She had witnessed the power of community, the importance of truth, and the necessity of justice. And she had come to understand that the story of The Great Return was not just about the past—it was about the future, about the kind of country England could become.

As she sat in her flat in London, looking out over the city that had been her home and her inspiration, Sarah felt a sense of fulfilment and purpose. The work of rebuilding and reconciliation was far from over, but it was a journey that she was proud to be a part of. The stories she had told were just the beginning, and she knew that there were many more stories to come—stories of hope, resilience, and the enduring human spirit.

The Great Return had been a moment of crisis, but it had also been a moment of opportunity. It had forced the country to confront its past, to face its deepest fears, and to begin the process of healing. The road ahead was long, but it was also filled with potential. England was beginning a new chapter in its history, one that would be written by the people who had come together in the face of adversity to build a better future. As Sarah prepared to start work on her next project, she felt a sense of excitement and anticipation. The journey of The Great Return was over, but the journey of renewal and transformation was just beginning. And as the sun set over the city, casting a golden glow over the skyline, Sarah knew that the best was yet to come.

As England stepped into a new possibility, Sarah was ready to continue telling the stories that would shape the nation's future.

Printed in Great Britain
by Amazon